I0818108

# WHITECHAPEL RISING

A John Decker Novel

ANTHONY M. STRONG

WEST STREET

# ALSO BY ANTHONY M. STRONG

## THE JOHN DECKER SUPERNATURAL THRILLER SERIES

Soul Catcher (prequel) • What Vengeance Comes • Cold Sanctuary

Crimson Deep • Grendel's Labyrinth • Whitechapel Rising

Black Tide • Ghost Canyon • Cryptic Quest • Last Resort

Dark Force • A Ghost of Christmas Past • Deadly Crossing

Final Destiny • Night Wraith

## THE CUSP FILES

Deadly Truth • Devil's Forest

## THE REMNANTS SERIES

The Remnants of Yesterday • The Silence of Tomorrow

## STANDALONE BOOKS

The Haunting of Willow House • Crow Song

## AS A.M. STRONG WITH SONYA SARGENT

**Patterson Blake FBI Mystery Series**

Never Lie To Me (Prequel) • Sister Where Are You

Is She Really Gone • All The Dead Girls

Never Let Her Go • Dark Road From Sunset

I Will Find Her

**Standalone Psychological Thrillers**

The Last Girl Left

# WHITECHAPEL RISING

West Street Publishing



Cover art and interior design by Bad Dog Media, LLC.

ISBN: 978-1-942207-14-6

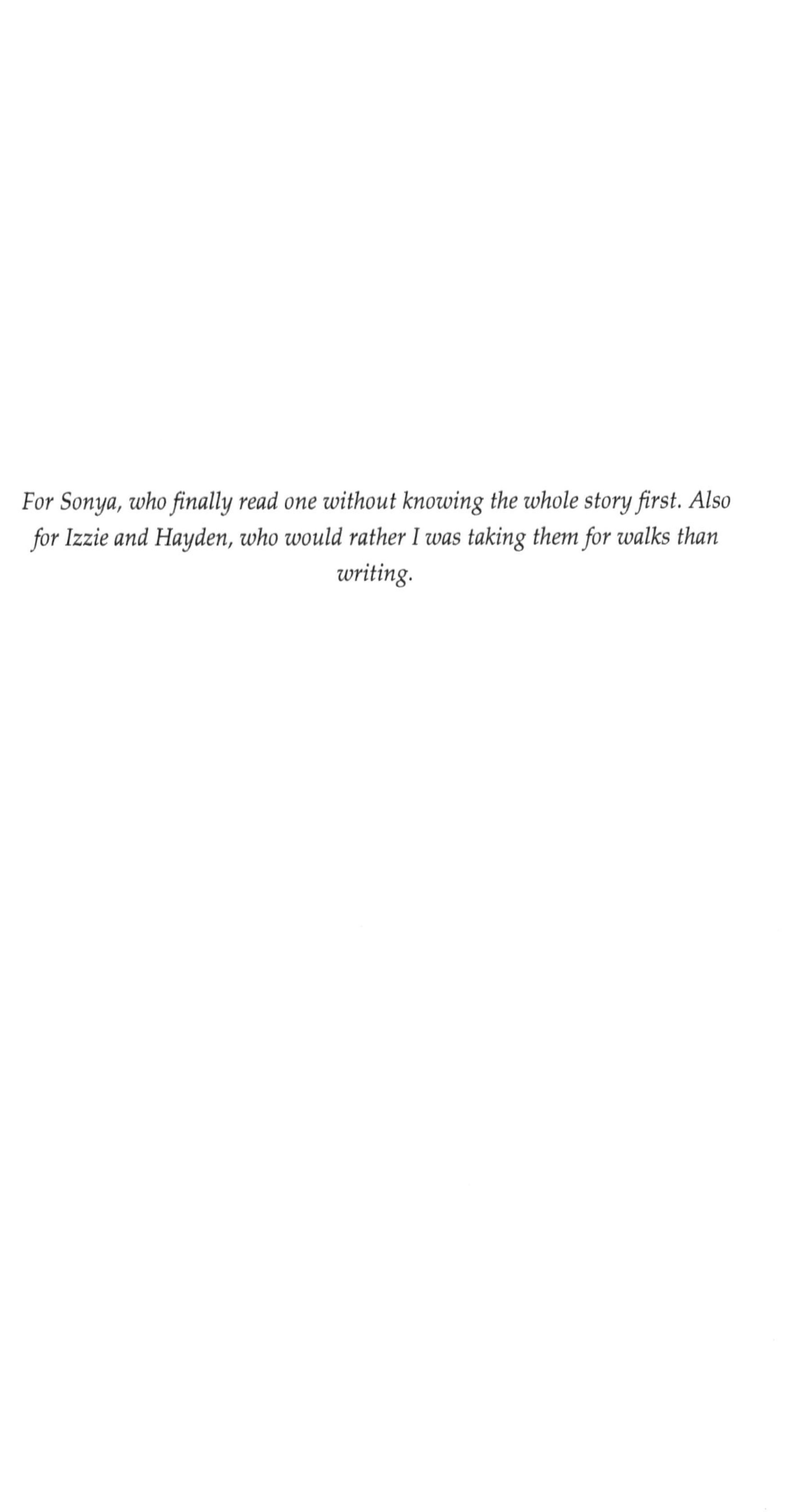

*For Sonya, who finally read one without knowing the whole story first. Also for Izzie and Hayden, who would rather I was taking them for walks than writing.*

CLASSIFIED UNIVERSAL SPECIAL PROJECTS
VERUM CONQUISITOR

# PROLOGUE

## THE WHITECHAPEL DISTRICT, LONDON – FEBRUARY 1889

THEY ARRIVED TOO late to save her. She lay in the doorway of a common lodging-house on Heneage Street, slumped over as if passed out from drink. This was not an unusual sight in the early hours of the morning on the foggy streets of Whitechapel, especially on a Friday when the dockworkers and laborers took their weekly pay in search of entertainment. Those wages, given over to the women of the night, were swiftly spent in the taverns and pubs thereabouts, even if that money would've been better spent renting a bed for the night. Except this woman was not sleeping off the fruits of her ill-gotten gains. The gash that opened her throat and sent blood spilling down the front of her dress bore testament to that.

When they came upon the scene, they found her attacker stooped over the body, a knife in one hand. With the other he gripped her hair and held his victim's head back so he could crouch low, his mouth upon the wound.

"Dear God. It looks like he's..." Frederick Abberline didn't finish the remark, his voice trailing off in horror.

"Yes, precisely. He appears to be licking the wound." Thomas

Finch, formerly of her Majesty's Grenadier Guards, spoke in a hushed voice even though they were standing in the entrance to a brewer's yard and out of earshot.

"We should apprehend the scoundrel now, while he's in the act." Abberline took a determined step forward.

Finch extended an arm and held him back. "Not so fast, Inspector. We cannot bring him in, you know that. We need a more permanent solution."

"A cell in Newgate followed by a date with the noose feels permanent enough to me," Abberline said.

"Might I remind you, Inspector, that I am in charge." Finch spoke the words with the assurance of one comfortable in their authority. "And if you would take exception to that, do so with her Majesty, Queen Victoria, herself."

"That won't be necessary." If Inspector Abberline felt slighted by this challenge to his rank, he showed no such emotion. Instead, he nudged his companion and nodded toward the doorway. "He's on the move."

"Then we shall follow," Finch said. He did his best to commit the man's features to memory-heavy coat, button-over boots, and derby hat-lest they temporarily lose sight of him. "But we must keep our distance. We cannot alert him to our presence."

"I've been hunting this animal for months," Abberline said as they stepped out of the shadows. He picked up a black leather satchel. "And now that we've caught him in the act, all we're going to do is trail behind as he makes his escape. It doesn't sit right with me. Think of the cases I could close if we make an arrest."

"There will be no arrest tonight." Finch pulled his jacket tight against the biting February chill. He understood Inspector Abberline's frustration. Only a few months earlier, his own inclination would have been the same. Throw the deviant in jail and let him rot to the end of his days. But in the time since, his sentiment had changed. There were monsters in this world, savage beasts that required a firmer hand, and this was one of them. Finch leaned close to Abberline, his breath misting the air. "He will not kill again; of that I assure you."

"I hope you're right."

"I am." They approached the doorway, and the sprawled woman within. Finch kneeled and pulled a handkerchief from his coat pocket. He reached to her neck and soaked a good amount of the blood into the cloth. "The bag. Quickly."

The inspector opened the bag to allow Finch to deposit the handkerchief inside, then closed it again. This done, he reached toward the victim's wrist to check for a pulse.

"Leave her. We don't have time." Finch stood and steered his companion away from the grisly scene. He felt a pang of sorrow. Minutes ago, this poor soul had been a living human being with years ahead of her, albeit bleak. Now she was nothing more than a lifeless, limp rag doll sitting in a widening pool of her own blood. It wasn't fair. But then, little was fair in the teeming slums of East London. He placed a reassuring hand on the inspector's shoulder. "Besides, there's nothing you can do for her now. She's beyond our help."

"We could at least have checked."

"That would have achieved nothing except allowing her killer to escape into the mist yet again." Finch said. "I assure you she's dead."

"I hate this job sometimes." Abberline blew on his hands for warmth. He kept pace with Finch and together they followed their quarry along Brick Lane, and then Fournier Street.

At Spitalfields Market, the man paused. Finch saw him reach under his coat and remove a fob watch. He glanced at it, then slipped the watch back inside the coat's folds. Now he lingered at the curb, as if he had not a care in the world, looking more like a gentleman out for a late evening stroll than a frenzied killer.

"What's he doing?" Abberline asked.

"I don't know," Finch replied, perplexed. There were few people on the streets at such a late hour, and they were still close to the murder scene. Their quarry should not be so confident in his escape. If a constable out patrolling the streets came across the body, the entire area would swarm with uniformed police in a matter of minutes. The city had been holding its breath, waiting for another murder since the gruesome discovery of Mary Kelly in her lodgings the previous

November. Finch knew that Abberline had attended that crime scene. He also knew the great restraint it was taking for the Inspector not to blow his whistle and bring the uniforms running to make an arrest.

A moment later they had their answer.

A black carriage pulled up, obstructing their view of the murderer. When it pulled away again, their target had vanished.

"Damn it all." Abberline ran into the street and watched the departing carriage with a mixture of frustration and horror. "He's going to get away after all."

"Not tonight, he won't." Finch raised a hand and looked down the empty street in the opposite direction to that which the carriage was now receding.

"What are you doing?"

"You'll see." A second carriage came into view, appearing from a side street as if it had been waiting there all along. After it stopped Finch motioned to Abberline. "If you'd care to climb aboard, I believe we have a murderer to catch."

"How on earth did you do that?" Abberline asked as he heaved himself up into the carriage.

"Working for the Queen's new investigative division has its perks." Finch leaned forward and told the driver to get moving. "Our resources far outstrip that of the Metropolitan police."

"But even so…" Abberline appeared flabbergasted. As the carriage gave chase, he glanced toward Finch. "You know, you haven't told me who you actually work for. All I received was an order from Sir Charles to follow your instructions without question."

"If the Commissioner gave you those orders, then why are you questioning me?"

"I just thought-"

"That your curiosity was getting the better of you?" Finch pulled his window down and leaned out, the breeze tussling his hair as he watched the pursuit.

The first carriage was following a weaving path through the streets, turning left, then right, and left again, only to arrive back upon the street it had originally been following. Finch guessed the circuitous route was meant to confuse anyone who noticed the speeding vehicle. He surmised, however, that they were heading for Mayfair given the general direction of travel. Ten minutes later he received confirmation of this hunch when the carriage finally came to a halt outside a three-story townhouse on Hay's Mews.

Finch tapped on the carriage window and instructed their own driver to continue on past the Mews before stopping out of sight. They disembarked and hurried back to the corner in time to see the man in the derby hat disappear into the townhouse.

"We've got him now." There was a tinge of excitement in Abberline's voice. "He won't be ripping any more women."

"If all goes well, you are correct." Finch led his companion toward the townhouse, stepping aside as the Ripper's carriage trundled past, empty now. When they reached the building Finch stopped. He glanced down toward the satchel that the inspector clutched in his hand. "We should prepare."

"Right-ho." Abberline kneeled and rested the satchel on the floor. He undid the buckles and opened it, withdrawing a bone handled Bowie knife with a ten-inch blade. This he handed to Finch. He withdrew a second knife and placed it on the ground near the bag.

"What about the rest of it?" Finch asked. He weighed the knife in one hand and touched the thumb of the other to the blade to satisfy himself of its sharpness.

"I have everything right here." Abberline withdrew a set of accordion bellows of the type used to fan the flames in a fireplace. They would use this set for a much darker and important purpose. Next, he withdrew the sodden bloodstained handkerchief. Finally, he removed a set of Darby handcuffs that glinted a pale yellow under the weak light from a nearby gas lamp. "Tell me again why these need to be solid gold?"

"We've been through this already."

"Seems a shame to waste so much precious metal."

"It's the only way." Finch held his hand out. "Give me the cuffs and handkerchief."

Abberline complied, before picking up his Bowie knife and the bellows. He stood up, leaving the satchel on the pavement. If they survived this night, he would retrieve it later. "We'd best get this over with then."

"You know what to do?"

Abberline nodded.

"Good." Finch approached the townhouse door before glancing back at his partner. "Remember to keep a cool head in there. We need no more deaths tonight."

"I'll keep my head," Abberline said, then he squared himself to the door, and kicked it in with a heavy boot.

It had begun.

# ONE

## MAYFAIR, LONDON – TWO DAYS AGO

REGGIE BRADSHAW STOOD, hands on hips and looked up at the three-floor townhouse in the affluent London suburb of Mayfair with a scowl on his face.

"How do people afford these places?" He asked with a shake of his head. "I swear the rich keep getting richer and the poor get poorer. It ain't fair."

"Has it ever been fair?" His co-worker, Matthew Kent, was used to Reggie's diatribes about class inequality and the plowing asunder of the workingman. He'd be lying if he said it didn't get old. "Pays our wages though," he added, hoping Reggie would drop the subject, just this once.

"Only because we were the cheapest bid. Tight arsed bastards." Reggie couldn't imagine what it would be like to occupy such a fancy property in the middle of the city. His own palatial spread was a four-room flat on the Marsden Estate in Acton, and that included the bathroom. The local authorities had earmarked the tower block for demolition three years before, then changed their minds. This did nothing but ensure the council-owned estate received even less maintenance than before. Now there was fresh talk of tearing the fifteen-story eyesore down, and Reggie hoped they did, because then he might get moved to a nicer council house in the suburbs. Somewhere with a garden. Either way, he wouldn't get to live anywhere near the multimillion pound homes he helped renovate for the stockbrokers and company directors that swarmed London's financial and business districts. It was, he thought, depressing.

"Come on, then. If you're done with grumbling, we should get to work." Matthew lifted his toolbox from the back of the van. With the other hand, he grabbed a small jackhammer and started toward the empty and partially gutted building. "I'd like to get out of here at a reasonable time tonight, I've got better things to do with my evening than working for the man."

"Like what?" Reggie scooped up his own toolbox and an angle grinder, slammed the van's back doors, then followed his partner into the townhouse and down what remained of the home's main hallway. To his left a twisting staircase climbed upward into darkness, the exposed support studs giving it the appearance of a skeletal snake coiling through the building's innards. "All you ever do is sit on your fat behind, eat pizza, and watch TV. When you're not sinking a few at the pub, that is."

"Yeah. Like your life's a whirl of society events." People who lived in glass houses shouldn't throw stones, as the tired old phrase went. "If you must know, I have a date."

Reggie almost creased over with laughter. "You realize the woman who serves you at the chip shop on Dean Road doesn't count as a date, right?"

"Eff off." Matthew gave his partner the middle finger as they reached the door leading to the cellar.

"Do you stare into each other's eyes over a nice piece of fried haddock?" Reggie chuckled at his own wit and flipped the light switch, then started down the steps.

"You're in the wrong profession, mate," Matthew said as they reached the bottom. "You should've become a standup comedian."

"I'd have been damned good at it too." Reggie placed his toolbox on the floor and switched on a set of halogen work lamps aimed toward a brick wall near the back of the cellar. The twin beams illuminated a weaving step crack that ran from the bottom of the wall to the joists above. Nearby, a pair of hydraulic jacks supported the ceiling. This would allow them to chip out the old bricks and mortar and rebuild the wall without the entire structure coming down on their heads.

"What are you in the mood for today?" Matthew asked, heading for an old boombox. Covered in multicolored flecks of paint and an unhealthy layer of dust, the thing had seen better days. He shuffled through a pile of CDs. "We have some Madonna, Aerosmith, and Rick Astley."

"Why on earth do we have Rick Astley?" Reggie plugged the handheld jackhammer into an extension cord and approached the wall. "Do I look like a teenaged girl from 1989? You'll be telling me you have a Right Said Fred CD next."

Matthew shrugged. "Don't ask me, they aren't mine, I found them in the van. I don't even own any CDs. Gave them all to the charity shop years ago when I got into the streaming and all that. Purely digital, I am."

"You're purely something."

"Just pick one. It doesn't matter much, anyway; we won't hear it for shit over that jackhammer."

"Might as well put on the Rick Astley then." Reggie donned a pair of ear protectors, then took a step toward the wall and pushed the jackhammer's blade against the mortar between the bricks. He tensed his arms and pulled the trigger a moment after the jangling refrain of "never gonna give you up" filled the cellar. The ear-splitting thrum of the hardened steel bit smacking into the cement holding the bricks in place did a fine job of drowning out the questionable music. He sensed Matthew standing to his left, watching the jackhammer chip away at the wall. When his arms got tired, he would stop and hand the tool over to his partner. They would keep this up, switching back and forth, until the old brickwork was removed, and a new, stronger wall replaced it.

It didn't take as long as they thought.

After only a few minutes of pounding with the jackhammer, Reggie noticed a spider's web of new cracks spiraling out from the original and following the lines of mortar that held the century-old bricks together.

He felt Matthew tap his shoulder, the touch urgent. Then, before he could even let his finger up from the jackhammer's trigger, the wall in front of him heaved and buckled, then came crashing down in a billowing cloud of dust.

"Holy hell," Reggie jumped backwards just in time to avoid the debris. The jackhammer ceased its incessant chatter.

Matthew coughed and waved a hand in front of his face to disperse the cloying dust that hung in the air. "Sweet. That didn't take as long as I thought it would."

"Damned wall almost got me." Reggie set the jackhammer aside and kicked at a stray brick that had landed near his foot. "Whole thing must've been rotten. It's a wonder it didn't come down on its own."

The dust was settling now. Matthew wiped a particle from his eye and peered at the yawning hole revealed by the collapsed wall. The halogen lamp lit enough of the space beyond to reveal that they had found another room. "Will you look at that?"

"No wonder this wall was failing. It's not original to the building. Is not even part of the foundation." Reggie inched forward, stepping gingerly over the collapsed bricks. He reached out and touched the hole's vertical edges where the newer brickwork had, until a few moments ago, met the old. "This used to be a doorway. Someone must've bricked it up at some point."

"I've heard about this kind of stuff," Matthew said. "There was this pub over in Hackney where they found a whole tunnel system behind a basement wall. There's probably places like this all over the city."

"Question is, what's in there." Reggie nodded toward the work lamp sitting on its tripod a few feet away. "Bring that thing over here, let's see what we've got."

"Maybe there's treasure back there." Matthew lifted the lamp by its handle and started toward the hole.

"It's a bricked-up room, dumbass." Reggie rolled his eyes. "Why would there be treasure? You think some stray Victorian pirate wandered down here with his chest of gold coins?"

"There must be something valuable in that room, otherwise, why would they hide it?" Matthew set the lamp down in front of the newly exposed entrance.

"Let's find out." Reggie stepped beyond the opening. The room was large, falling away into darkness beyond the halogen work light's beams. It was, he guessed, at least a third the size of the cellar they'd been working in.

"Wow." Matthew had his phone out, the flashlight pushing back the gloom. He played the beam over the walls to expose a yellowed map of Whitechapel with curled edges that sagged in one corner where the pin holding it had rusted away. Next to this, in the same deteriorated condition, were newspaper clippings also attached to the wall, front pages with dramatic headlines in fading ink. *Horror in Whitechapel. Jack slaughters Two in One Night.* East End *Ripper Claims a Fifth Victim.*

"Look at this. You're never going to believe it," Reggie said from further within the room.

Matthew turned away from the wall.

Reggie had his own phone out, it's light playing over a wooden table. There, glinting in the beam from his flashlight, was a vicious-looking knife, the tarnished blade stained dark in patches. "I think that's blood. You don't think we've found…" Reggie's voice trailed off.

"Jack the Ripper's lair?" Matthew could hardly believe what he was seeing.

"Yeah."

"I don't know." Matthew lifted his phone, shining the light beyond the table. "But if we have, then *that* must be Jack himself."

Reggie looked up, a chill running through him when he saw what Matthew was looking at. There, caught in the beam of his coworker's light, was a corpse. It was sitting on a chair in the furthest recesses of the room, hands behind its back, a rictus grin painted across taut skin the color of varnished mahogany. Clearly male, it wore a shirt once white, the fabric now stained with splotches in varying degrees of brown. Dusty hair clung to its scalp, dull black and wiry. The corpse was in a remarkable state of preservation considering how long it must have been there. Even its eyes were open, looking at him with a dead, milky stare.

Reggie shuddered and took a step backwards.

An image flitted through his mind. The corpse climbing to its feet and lurching toward them, exhaling wispy puffs of dust as it cleared its desiccated lungs.

Reggie resisted the urge to turn and flee back up the stairs and not stop until he was in the street. Instead, he looked at Matthew, a grim expression on his face. "I think we'd better call the police."

# TWO

HAY'S MEWS had been a circus of police and forensic technicians all afternoon. Even though the cadaver in the cellar had been there for decades, it still required the authorities to confirm no crime had taken place, at least not in any timeframe worth investigating. Now, as dusk settled across the city, there were only two vehicles left. A white van labeled as a private ambulance, waiting to receive the body, and a cherry red FIAT Uno that belonged to a team of researchers from the University of Central London who had spent the last four hours cataloging the hidden room and examining the contents within.

Rebecca Langley, the ambulance's driver, leaned in the doorway the collapsed bricks had revealed and watched the university people fuss about snapping photos, taking measurements, and conversing in hushed tones. Her coworker, Anil, had given up and wandered off, and was no doubt on the phone chatting to his girlfriend out by the van.

Rebecca yawned, bored now the excitement of standing inside Jack the Ripper's dungeon of horrors had worn off. When they'd shown up earlier that afternoon, she'd expected this to be a quick scoop and run. Grab the body and drop it off at the Westminster Public Mortuary, the closest facility to Mayfair. That was hours ago. Her shift should've ended already, and it irked her she was wasting her evening on this, despite the overtime pay. She had plans. Right now she should be at Jacque's with her husband, enjoying a glass of chardonnay and a plate of seared scallops. The French restaurant was notoriously hard to book, with a waiting list that stretched weeks. Instead, she was standing in a dusty basement while their reservation went to some lucky walk-in, and her husband ate a microwave meal in front of the telly. For sure, this would make for a wonderful story down the road, when the frustration of missing date night had worn off. As it was, she couldn't even tell her husband about it. There was a media blackout on the startling discovery, at least until the authorities processed the scene and removed the body. The last thing anyone wanted was a horde of over-eager reporters and slack-jawed gawkers descending on the townhouse. Not that the discovery would stay a secret for long. In her experience, someone always leaked to the press. It was only a matter of time before eager journalists showed up with their news vans, at least until some other shiny story caught their attention.

Something was happening. There was a definite rise in the tension that permeated the dank cellar. One researcher, a mousy woman with straw blonde cropped hair who had introduced herself as Callie, called out to her assistant, voice heavy with excitement. "Martin, bring me a specimen bag, quick as you can."

A rail thin kid who looked barely old enough to be out of school turned from his study of the bloodied knife on the desk and whipped a plastic bag from an evidence kit sitting on the floor.

He handed it to his boss. "What do we have?"

"Some kind of dust here," Callie peered closely at the cadaver's face, and the brown skin stretched taut over it. "Like metal filings. If I didn't know better, I'd think it was gold."

"Just like the handcuffs." Martin glanced backwards toward a plastic tub within which sat most of the smaller loose items already photographed in situ. One of these, and the cause of flurried excitement half an hour previously, had been a set of golden restraints holding the corpse's wrists together behind its back. Originally the researchers had left them in place, but the mere act of probing caused the cuffs to drop off the emaciated body. When they picked the cuffs up it became obvious, because of their weight, that they were solid gold.

"This is getting stranger by the minute." Callie straightened up. "I think I've got all the metal particles from the face. We'll test them back at the university."

Rebecca wondered how much longer this was going to take. She might have missed her restaurant reservation, but she would still like to get home before midnight. She dug her hand into her trouser pocket and pulled out a packet of cigarettes, slipping one from the carton and lifting it toward her mouth.

"Excuse me." Callie was glaring in her direction. "You can't light that in here."

"Fine. I'll go outside. Just let me know when you're done." Rebecca stomped back through the cellar and up to the first floor, then made her way through the building and out into the street.

# THREE

HE DRIFTED into consciousness as a drowning man might kick toward the water's surface, desperate for air yet lost in a world of suffocating blackness. But then a pinprick of dull light appeared within the darkness as eyes that had stared blankly but hadn't seen for over a century began to work again.

Abraham Turner's chest heaved as he sucked a rasping breath into dry, desiccated lungs.

His vision had returned now, the void in which he'd slumbered retreating to reveal the familiar surroundings of the den hidden beneath his Mayfair residence. He opened his mouth, ran his tongue across lips as dry as sandpaper, and wondered if he dared move.

He felt old. Ancient.

He could sense the ravages of time weaving their way through his wasted muscles and mineralized bones. A thought flickered through his awakening brain. A memory of his last moments, or at least the last ones until now. Two men, one of whom he recognized, the other he did not. They had invaded his home. His sacred temple. And somehow, impossibly, they knew how to stop him.

A name rose through the fog.

Abberline.

Detective Inspector Frederick Abberline.

He felt a surge of rage as he remembered the inspector coming toward him, bellows in hand while at his side, the man with the glinting handcuffs.

Those restraints were now gone, as was the gold dust used to stun him into submission. Abberline was gone too. He did not know from where this knowledge flowed, only that the inspector was long departed. Nothing but dust and bones.

Abraham finally found the will to move. He clenched his fists, joints popping as stiff fingers curled around the chair's armrests. He raised himself up gingerly, making sure his legs could still bear weight.

The pain in his muscles was receding now, ebbing to a dull ache. He glanced around, dismayed to see that many of his prized possessions were missing, including the knife that had served him so well. He lifted a hand to his shirt, felt around for the fob watch that should still hang there. A tight knot of panic formed in his stomach when he didn't find it.

Gone. No doubt stolen by Abberline and his crony. An insurance policy should anyone ever free him from eternal slumber.

He stumbled forward on unsteady legs, heading toward the room's only entrance. He shielded his eyes from the bright light that shone from beyond the gaping hole and made his way toward the stairs. When he reached the first floor he paused.

His home, once opulent and comfortable, was now barely recognizable. Of his furnishings, there was no sign. The walls were gone, only a skeletal framework of wooden supports left. The stairs that rose to his second-floor bedchamber were in a similar state. Dust and debris littered the floor. Tools were strewn about, some of which he recognized, some he did not. One thing was obvious. This was not his home anymore. If he had been capable of sorrow, the sad state of his former residence would have elicited such an emotion, but he was not.

The front door stood open. From beyond he heard voices. Female. He felt a rush of adrenaline. The fob watch might be gone but he still felt the urge for blood. He glanced down at his wrist, and the intricate symbol burned into a circle there. Maybe he didn't need the watch.

Abraham lurched toward the door. He wished he had the knife, his reliable blade. He glanced around at the discarded tools for a suitable replacement. There, sitting atop a metal toolbox, he found it. A short-bladed knife of curious design. He picked it up and weighed it in his hand. The knife was unusually light; the handle contoured to fit his curling fingers, with a short thin blade little more than an inch long at the business end. It felt flimsy in his grip. Not a respectable weapon, but it would suffice for now.

He moved toward the door and paused, evaluating the situation. It was dark outside; the Mews swathed only in the weak light of streetlamps positioned at intervals. The chatter had ceased now. Two men and a woman were standing near a horseless carriage of strange design. Another carriage, this one bigger, sat directly in front of him at the curb. Further away he heard other voices, within which he recognized the abandonment of inebriation. The last time he'd left this building – how long ago that was, he had no idea – there had been a pub on the corner. Apparently, it was still there. He felt a surge of need, felt his body thirsting for the blood that would renew him and revitalize his wasted frame. It took all of his willpower to turn away from the group near the horseless carriage. This street was too busy. He needed a better victim. A lone victim.

Abraham turned away and bowed his head lest anyone see him and shuffled off down the street as quick as his stiff legs would allow. He stepped into the road to cross to the other side and avoid the rowdy pub. He'd barely taken three steps when a sudden squeal rent the air. Blinding light flared around him. Abraham raised his arms to shield his face and saw one of the monstrous horseless carriages swerving away. As it drew level, a face appeared at the side window, brow creased in anger.

"Get out of the road, moron!" The driver lifted a hand and made a gesture that Abraham didn't understand, and then the vehicle was disappearing into the night, rear lights glowing red like a pair of demonic eyes.

Abraham stood there a moment, bewildered. How long had he been sleeping? What was this strange new world with vehicles that ran like trackless railroad engines, but without the steam? He would find out soon enough, of that he was sure. First, though, he had a more pressing need. Up ahead was an alley between two buildings and walking toward it from the direction of the pub, a little unsteady on her feet, a slender girl of perhaps twenty years of age. He watched her enter the alley. The darkness swallowed her up.

Abraham smiled, or at least it would have been a smile if the stiff mummified skin stretched across his skull had allowed it. And now it didn't matter how many years had passed, because tonight, the ripping would begin anew.

# FOUR

WHEN REBECCA EXITED THE TOWNHOUSE, Anil was sitting in the van, a phone up to his ear. She could see his wide shoulders and the outline of his head through the tinted side window. As she suspected he was chatting to his girlfriend, oblivious to the world around him.

Rebecca walked around the back of the van and leaned against the side facing the street. On the opposite pavement, a potbellied man with a receding hairline was watching his boxer dog push one out. Once finished he strolled off without bothering to pick the mess up, the animal straining on its leash. Nice, Rebecca thought. Leave it there for someone to step in.

She put the cigarette to her lips and lit it, sucking back a stream of nerve calming smoke. She closed her eyes and exhaled; happy to be out of the claustrophobic and moldy cellar. Sounds of laughter drifted from further down the street. A cluster of university lads were leaving the King's Head pub on the corner and weaving their way off down Hill Street. She watched them go with a measure of envy and wondered if anyone would notice if she left her post and sneaked into the pub for half a lager. But of course, she would not do that. There was a job to do. A body to drop at the mortuary if those researchers ever got their butts moving and let her and Anil collect it. Still, it was nice to fantasize. There was a partially drunk bottle of cheap plonk at home sitting on the kitchen counter, the remains of yesterday evening's fun, and after her shift finished, it would be an empty bottle. Not as good as the Chardonnay at Jacque's, or a cold half pint in the pub, but it would suffice. She was still pondering this when footsteps approached.

"All done." Callie, the blonde-haired researcher, appeared from behind the van. "You can bring our happy chappie down there over to the mortuary at the university medical school. There will be someone there to greet you and take possession at the entrance on Arthur Street."

"Medical school? I thought he was going to Westminster. The university's all the way over the other side of the city."

"Sorry." Callie shrugged. "We need to get him into a controlled environment as soon as possible for preservation." She grinned. "Can you believe we found Jack the Ripper? This is so awesome."

"Yeah, it's a dream come true," Rebecca said without trying to hide her sarcasm.

"Okay then." Callie hesitated as if she was trying to sum Rebecca up, then she retreated and joined her colleagues who were lifting a hard-sided plastic tub full of artifacts into the FIAT. That done, they climbed in and slammed the doors. Moments later, the car pulled away from the curb, performing a U-turn in the street.

Rebecca watched the vehicle drive past and take a left at the end of the road, disappearing from sight. She shook her head in disbelief. This was just great. Now instead of a fifteen-minute drive to the Westminster mortuary, she would have to hightail it all the way across town like some kind of morbid pizza delivery boy, dropping the corpse off for the university eggheads to fawn over.

Well, screw them.

They could wait for their precious body until she was good and ready to move it. Her evening was ruined anyway, so why bother rushing.

She took another long drag of the cigarette, blowing the smoke out in a lazy stream that caught the breeze and twisted away before dissipating.

Another car turned onto the Mews, its headlights painting her in a brilliant white glare as it did so. She glanced toward it, wondering if the researchers had forgotten something and were returning, but it wasn't them. It was bigger, an SUV with a roof rack.

The car swerved to avoid a figure crossing the road. A drunkard fresh from the pub on the corner, most likely. It slowed. The window rolled down. The driver shouted an angry remark at the weaving pedestrian, then sped up again, passing Rebecca and continuing down the street before turning at the other end. When she looked back, the solitary figure had vanished.

Rebecca took a last drag of the cigarette and dropped the butt, grinding it under her heel, then walked around the van and banged on the passenger window inches from Anil's head. She'd wasted enough time to prove her point. Might as well get this over with.

"What the…" Anil jumped. He threw her a withering look before opening the door and climbing out. "You scared the shit out of me."

"Maybe if you were paying attention, I wouldn't need to." Rebecca jerked her thumb toward the building. "Grab the gurney, we have our passenger."

Anil went to the back of the van and dragged out the gurney, dropping the retractable legs. He wheeled it toward the townhouse and through the front door. When they reached the cellar stairs, he retracted the legs again, and they carried it down into the bowels of the building.

"Sure is spooky down here," Anil said, glancing around. The worker's halogen light was still on, but it didn't have the power to push away the furthest shadows. "Doesn't help that we are literally inside the domain of the world's most elusive serial killer. You can feel the evil down here."

"Don't be so dramatic." Rebecca tried to laugh off the comment, but she could feel it too. A palpable heaviness pushing down as if she were walking through the soul of the building itself.

Anil picked his way through the rubble of the fallen wall. He stepped into the secret chamber and flicked the gurney's legs down once more, wheeling it into the room. Then he stopped and looked around. "What are we supposed to be picking up down here?"

"The corpse, moron. It's kind of hard to miss," Rebecca said, climbing through the hole in the wall and joining her partner.

"You sure they didn't take it with them already?" Anil scratched his head, confused.

"In a FIAT Uno? What you think they did, strap it to the roof?"

"Maybe. Because it isn't down here."

"What are you talking about?" Rebecca snapped, but even as she said the words, she realized Anil was right. The chair the corpse had sat on for the last hundred and thirty years was now empty. Jack was gone.

# FIVE

HE FOLLOWED her into the alley, keeping a safe distance as she weaved along, humming a tune under her breath. He didn't want her to know he was there. Not just yet. He needed time to ready himself. He was slow, unsure on his feet. Before his brush with Abberline, when he was stalking the streets of Whitechapel, his victims never knew what hit them. They were easy prey. Half the time he didn't even need to follow them. He just found them passed out from drink in a doorway, their breath reeking of gin.

Already he could tell this was a different time. Everything was brighter and cleaner. And the people, those that he had seen so far, looked nothing like the wretched souls that had inhabited his old stalking grounds. One thing hadn't changed. The air still stank. It was not the black sooty smog that filled Victorian streets, but it was no less offensive. An invisible odor that belched from the horseless carriages which now filled the roads. Not that he cared. His lungs were far beyond being damaged by any pollutant man could create, and soon, when he spilled blood again, they would rejuvenate, his muscles strengthen, and his skin lose the pallor of death. He would become human again, or at least as human as he had ever been.

He could see the end of the alley up ahead. The woman was still humming as she walked, her shoes making clicking sounds on the concrete as she went. He didn't have much time if he wanted to do this out of sight.

He hurried his own step, gripping the knife in his hand, and slipping up behind her soundlessly. He hadn't lost his touch. She never even knew he was there. At least until he snaked an arm around her neck and brought it back in a jerking motion, the knife's small blade digging deep into the skin under her chin and silencing her scream before it even began.

Her hands flew to her throat. She turned around, eyes wide with terror. Blood was pushing through her fingers now, hot and fast, even as she gazed upon the nightmare face of her attacker. A visage summoned from hell itself.

She opened her mouth, but any capacity to talk had escaped along with the blood that now soaked her top under the light jacket she wore. She stumbled backwards, even now trying to escape as the life drained from her ruined neck. She pawed at the wound as if she could somehow push it back together, but even as she did so, her legs gave way and she sank to the ground. She sat there with her back against the alley wall, eyes pleading for help from the very man who had inflicted her mortal wound.

Abraham kneeled in front of the swiftly fading woman and placed a finger to his lips. 'It's okay,' he tried to say, soothing her into death. 'Your sacrifice will make me strong.' He wanted this pathetic creature to know that her death would not be in vain, that she would expire for some higher purpose. But instead of his carefully chosen words, all that came out was a dry rattle. His own vocal cords, it would appear, worked no better than his victim's recently severed cords. He found this frustrating. On top of it all, after being hunted down and incapacitated for such a long time, waking up to find his house desecrated, and an unfamiliar world beyond his front door, now he could not even speak. He felt a surge of anger rise into his throat like bile. He pulled the woman's hands from her neck even as she shook her head in a last-ditch attempt to stop him. Then he brought the knife down again, digging deeper this time, opening the wound wider. His old knife would've been better, more graceful, but this one got the job done, albeit with crude inefficiency.

She wouldn't last much longer. He could see the consciousness fading from her eyes. Another moment and her soul would flee. He placed the knife on the ground and dropped his head toward her, his mouth finding her neck, tongue probing the torn flesh it found there.

He withdrew and held his arm up to expose the symbol burned on the inside above the wrist. He brought it to his mouth and ran his bloodied tongue over it, smearing his skin red.

Then he waited.

Nothing happened.

The blood just sat there atop the ancient symbol-a brand seared into his wrist so many generations ago-instead of being absorbed the way it usually was. And he knew why. This wasn't how the ritual worked. He needed his fob watch. Without it, Abraham realized, he would not receive a new lease on life, would not regenerate. The blood alone was not enough.

Abraham bowed his head for a moment, centering the furious rage that burned within. He would find the watch. It was out there, somewhere. It was not destroyed. He could sense as much, even if he didn't know where it was. The watch and he were eternally linked, joined in violence and bloodshed.

He rose and stepped away from the newly minted corpse. It was dangerous to stay here. He'd ended up in that cellar room because he got cocky. Over-confident. He'd started enjoying the slaughter a bit too much. He wouldn't make the same mistake again. This time he would be more careful…

# SIX

## SOUTHERN IRELAND - NOW

JOHN DECKER SAT in the front passenger seat of CUSP's Land Rover as it sped through the Irish countryside. Next to him, in the driver's seat, was Adam Hunt, while Colum, the ex-Irish Army Ranger - still nursing a dislocated shoulder - sat in the back with Rory. Their destination was Dublin Airport. Decker and Colum to catch a flight to London's Heathrow, while Adam and Rory would take the private jet back to the States.

Decker sat with a newspaper on his lap. Across the top, a bold headline.

*Workers Renovating Mayfair Home Find Jack the Ripper's Lair! Murderer's Corpse Stolen.*

He'd already read the associated article three times, digesting as much useful information as he could from the sensationalized and dramatic piece to which most of the column inches on the front page were dedicated. Now he glanced toward Hunt.

"Intriguing as this is, I'm not sure what it has to do with us," Decker said. "I know you like to keep things close to the chest, but you've barely given us any information. If we're going to catch the people who took the body, we'll need something to go on."

"I never said that was your mission," Hunt replied with his usual lack of expression.

"Then what is the mission, boss?" Colum asked from the back seat.

"All in good time. First, you need a little background." Hunt paused for a few moments as if gathering his thoughts. When he continued, his voice was full of gravity. "There's a reason no one ever solved the Whitechapel murders. Jack the Ripper was no ordinary serial killer. He was a monster in the truest sense, stalking the streets of the city for his own amusement. Our predecessor, an organization called the Order of Saint George, spent months tracking him while he committed his heinous crimes. They finally caught up with him in the early months of 1889. He'd just finished his latest atrocity. Two agents working for the order at the behest of Queen Victoria, a man named Thomas Finch, and Detective Inspector Abberline of Scotland Yard, brought his reign of terror to an end."

"Except Jack the Ripper was never caught. There isn't even any real consensus regarding his identity." Colum was leaning forward now, his interest piqued. "Unless you're telling me that a hundred and thirty years of history is wrong."

"You've worked for us long enough to know that common knowledge isn't always correct knowledge," Hunt replied with an enigmatic smile. "But yes, you are correct. History did not record the true course of events."

"So, what happened?" Decker asked.

"Finch and Abberline followed him to his place of refuge and there they subdued him and walled him up in an underground chamber so he could never kill again."

"The room the renovation crew discovered." Decker glanced down at the newspaper again.

"Precisely. The room was his lair. Hidden under his house, the doorway was disguised by a rack of false shelves, or so the story goes."

"He wasn't dead, I assume," Decker said. "Otherwise, why bother walling him up."

"You are correct. He was not dead, at least not in the truest sense. Much like Grendel, whom we've recently dispatched to the Zoo, the Ripper was long lived and hard to kill. Except in this case he gained his longevity from the blood of his victims."

Colum snorted. "Are you sending us on a vampire hunt?"

"I'm not sure vampire is the right word. He did not drink the blood of his victims. But none-the-less, Jack and his kind have vampiric qualities and are, I'm certain, the true basis of the legends."

"Speaking of the Zoo, why didn't you move him there?" Decker asked. He'd only learned of CUSP's high-security facility where they kept the most dangerous creatures they captured a few days before. "It would seem risky to leave him out in the world."

"I agree, and under normal circumstances we would have moved him there as soon as the facility was available." Hunt kept his eyes on the road. They were approaching the city now, the traffic growing heavier with each mile. "Like I said, we did not directly stop the Ripper. It was the organization that came before us, founded in England by Queen Victoria in the year 1879. CUSP only came into existence during the Second World War as a collaboration between that organization and a fledgling American effort to thwart the Nazi's occult and supernatural leanings. It was also during that conflict when all records pertaining to Jack were lost, along with most of the other cases prior to the era, when an incendiary bomb destroyed the building which housed them, reducing it to fiery rubble."

"In other words, you know they walled Jack the Ripper up under a house in London, but you misplaced the address."

"That's a rather simplistic summary of the situation, but a fair one."

"And now someone stumbled upon it and released him."

"Precisely. The Ripper is one of a few cases that has remained on our radar over the decades. There was always a chance someone would discover his makeshift prison. We only hoped that he would remain dormant long enough for us to transport him to the Zoo."

"Well, that didn't happen." Colum reached over toward Decker's newspaper and pointed to a smaller headline underneath the Ripper story.

*Murder Shocks Mayfair.*
*Woman Found with Throat Slashed.*

"I'd bet any money, your vampire committed that murder," Colum said.

"I'd rather not call him a vampire," Hunt replied wearily. "He might sustain his life with blood, but his modus operandi is entirely different. He doesn't bite his victim's necks to drink their blood."

"No. Instead, he slashes them open with a knife to get to it, which somehow feels worse."

"Which is why the pair of you are going to London to stop him."

"Is there anything else you can tell us?" Decker said. "Anything that would help us find him?"

"I wish there were. We don't even know what he looks like, or even his actual name," Hunt said. They were on the approach road to the airport now. He followed the signs for departures. "I'll do some digging once I get Stateside, run a records search. Maybe there will be something that can help, but I wouldn't hold your breath."

"Okay then," Decker said as they pulled up outside of the terminal. "Off we go on another monster hunt."

# SEVEN

THE ABANDONED WORKHOUSE STOOD on a patch of overgrown scrubland in Bethnal Green, surrounded by wire fencing that had, itself, fallen into disrepair. Rain poured in, cascading past the wooden beams that used to support the roof, and drenching rooms and corridors now open to the elements.

Abraham Turner huddled in the remains of a dormitory closet, now one of the few places in the rambling old building that still offered some measure of shelter. Above him, in the crumbing rafters, birds flapped about. These were not the building's only occupants. Rats, their pink noses twitching, had scurried past him several times during the previous thirty-six hours. One particularly bold rodent had even veered into Abraham's makeshift shelter and sat on its hind legs, red eyes studying him. It was the diminutive creature's last earthly act. Abraham hadn't eaten since staggering from the townhouse cellar in Mayfair, and he could feel the hunger gnawing at his insides. He'd reached out toward the hapless creature and scooped it up, even as he expected it to dart away. But the rat hadn't attempted to flee. It was, Abraham reflected, as if the pitiful rodent were knowingly sacrificing itself so he might live. In return, Abraham dealt the rat a swift death, and then devoured it with gleeful abandon, wrenching the fur back to expose the raw meat beneath and picking the bones clean before discarding the carcass. The meal, unpalatable as it was, had provided some much-needed energy. But it was a temporary fix that didn't address the core problem.

What he needed was the fob watch.

The girl whose throat he'd cut in the alley had died in vain. Her blood, which should have rejuvenated and restored him, had done no such thing. After hundreds of years keeping himself young and agile by stealing the life force of others, he now faced the unenviable position of withering away, his body becoming a barely functional husk within which his consciousness would be trapped. At least until it crumbled away to nothing many long centuries from now and finally released his tortured spirit. And all because Frederick Abberline, and the unknown man who had accompanied him, somehow subdued Abraham, took the watch and entombed him. They had possessed knowledge far beyond that of simple police officers. They had known what he was, and how to render him incapable, even if they could not destroy him. His only comfort was that both men were surely long dead. Abraham now knew how much time had passed, having found a discarded newspaper blowing in the wind. A hundred and thirty years. He had spent more than a century down in that cellar while the world continued on around him. And what a world it now was. Brighter and cleaner than his own time, this new century brought its own evils. Like the horseless carriages that swarmed the streets belching pollutants as bad as any in his own day, even if their fumes were now invisible. There were other terrors, too. The previous morning, as he'd stayed hidden from the world in this wreck of a building, a mighty bird of man-made construction had flown low overhead with a terrible roar. At first, he hadn't known what it was, or where to look, but a glance skyward had revealed the metal-clad flying monstrosity. He wondered what other unknown wonders awaited him beyond the workhouse's crumbling walls. As soon as he figured out how to reclaim the watch, he would no doubt find out.

It was the watch, or rather the artifact contained within, that led him to the workhouse. He'd left the alley, keeping to the shadows lest anyone should see his dreadful and withered countenance. London had changed since he'd last trodden its streets. The roads were still there, most of them at least, but many of the familiar buildings were no longer standing. It was like some mighty hand had swept the city away and reimagined it. Rebuilt it from the ground up. He felt lost. Adrift.

After a while he grew tired of walking and found a bench. He sank down upon it, unsure where to go, or what to do next. Then, as he watched a vagrant wheel a grocery cart along the road, the basket piled high with black bags, old clothing, and unidentifiable detritus, he remembered the workhouse, and the man who ran it.

Erasmus White.

The Marsden Street workhouse had been a model of cruel efficiency in its heyday. Those unfortunate enough to end up within its walls – alcoholics, the unemployed, and the destitute – would have a bed waiting for them. But nothing was free. They would repay their night's slumber through backbreaking work and long hours. Many of these wretched souls were sent here against their will, imprisoned, sometimes for months on end, merely because they had the audacity to be poor. It was a hellish existence made worse by the unsanitary conditions that allow disease to run rampant. And lording over it all, with ruthless efficiency, was Erasmus White. Even if he had not been of Abraham's kind, he would have reveled in the cruelty he inflicted upon the inmates within his walls. As it was, they served another purpose. They were easy pickings. No one would miss a drunken lout, or a fallen woman pickled by gin. The workhouse became his market, and he chose his produce well. Even Abraham had occasionally used the workhouse when he needed an easy kill, although he preferred not to do this. Unlike Erasmus, he liked to be the hunter, stalking his prey through the darkened streets of the capital.

Now though, with his house gone and nowhere to rest his head, Abraham set out for Bethnal Green in search of his old friend, only to discover that the workhouse had fallen to rack and ruin. Of Erasmus White, there was no sign.

That was more than a day ago and Abraham had spent the time

since huddled out of sight in the abandoned building, unsure what to do next.

What he needed was the watch. Once he had that he would renew his ghastly appearance and extend his life for a while longer. Then he would assimilate back into society. If only he knew where the watch was. He could still sense it, calling out to him, but the signal was weak. He could not pinpoint its location. This led him to believe that Abberline, or his companion, had taken steps to shield the watch from him, realizing an unbreakable bond linked them. No matter. He would find it eventually. He had no doubts of that. In the meantime, he must preserve his strength until a suitable plan of action occurred to him. Abraham settled back into the filthy closet that had become his temporary home and closed his eyes. If another rat strayed close enough, he would have dinner. If not, he might as well get a few hours of sleep.

# EIGHT

THE FLIGHT to London was short and uneventful. Decker spent most of the duration with his head in a book about Jack the Ripper he had downloaded onto his tablet reader. At one point, upon reading that there were other victims associated with the Ripper, beyond the canonical five, he made a comment to Colum which went unanswered. When he glanced toward the burly Irishman, he discovered him to be sleeping, something Decker himself had always found hard to do on airplanes.

After landing and clearing customs, Decker and Colum caught a taxi directly to their accommodation. It was early afternoon, nowhere near rush hour, and already the traffic was a snarled nightmare in the center of the city. What should have been a short thirty-minute ride turned into two hours of bumper to bumper frustration, partly because of an accident on the M4 motorway that blocked one lane, pushing the creeping traffic into a bottleneck. When they eventually arrived, the afternoon was fast heading toward evening.

The Reardon Grand Hotel sat a block from Hyde Park and was within easy walking distance of the Ripper's lair on Hays Mews.

Now, after settling into their rooms and freshening up, Decker and Colum were sitting at a corner table in the hotel bar, far away from the few other patrons partaking of an evening drink. On the table in front of them was the report Adam Hunt had provided prior to their departure from Ireland.

"There's not much here," Decker said flicking through the thin stack of pages within the manila folder. "I'm not sure how he expects us to find the Ripper and subdue him with such a paltry amount of information to go on."

"Like the man said, the records relating to Jack's capture and imprisonment were lost during the second world war." Colum had ordered a pint and was already half through it. "This will not be a simple assignment."

"Neither was the last one," Decker said. He'd expected his first job with CUSP to be a stress-free frolic in the Irish countryside collecting some dusty old bones. Instead, it had turned into a showdown with the monster Grendel and his crazy, practically immortal mother. "I'm sure we'll figure it out."

"And even if we don't, at least we have excellent beer." Colum drained the last of his pint and pushed his chair back, standing up. He went to the bar and ordered another drink, then returned. As he took his seat again, he tapped the report. "Let's go over what we know so far."

"Well, we know Jack the Ripper was not a regular man. He was, if we are to believe Adam Hunt, a creature possessing vampiric qualities which enabled him to extend his life over an unknown span of time. To do this, he slit the throats of his victims, although he did not consume the blood in the manner associated with traditional vampires."

"We also know he was eventually stopped, although a German bomb in World War Two destroyed the records that could have told us precisely how."

"There has to be more to this than we're seeing," Decker said. "If Jack didn't drink the blood of those he killed, then what did he do with it?"

Colum shrugged and sipped his beer.

Decker continued. "Then there's the most recent murder. The

young woman found with her throat slashed in an alley not far from here."

"It's a fair bet that a recently freed Jack was the man responsible. The timeline coincides with his disappearance from the house on Hay's Mews."

"I agree. No sooner had Jack's body turned up missing, than a violent murder occurred less than two blocks away. The Ripper walked out of that cellar and went straight back to work doing what he does best."

"The question is, why have there been no subsequent murders?" Colum asked.

"Give him time. The Ripper may only need to kill infrequently to achieve his ends." Decker picked up his own drink, which he had ignored until now. "The sooner we find him the surer we can be of averting another death."

"If only we knew where to look," Colum said. "He could be anywhere in the city by now."

"Or he might have left the city already," Decker said. "Unlike the previous threats I've dealt with, this monster is intelligent. He surely realizes people will look for him."

"People who know that he's still alive." Colum leaned back in his chair. "So, where does that leave us?"

"Searching for a needle in a haystack," Decker replied. Finding one man within London's nine million residents would be next to impossible, even if Jack remained within the city's limits. "The first thing we need to do is find his true identity. That may give us a clue regarding his current movements."

"It's worth a try." Colum nodded. "We can start by looking at property records, see who owned that building on Hay's Mews in Victorian times. A man who's lived for centuries would surely leave a long trail."

"Assuming he kept the same identity throughout."

"True. But it's a place to start."

"Electoral and census records might turn up some useful information too," said Decker.

"We should be able to look that stuff up online," Colum replied. "There must be physical archives too if we can't find what we need on the web."

"Agreed."

"You want to get started then?" Colum finished off his pint. "We can't do much else tonight anyway. We might as well do some digging on the web. After we eat, of course. I'm starving."

"Me too," Decker admitted.

"Dinner it is then." Colum made a motion to stand up. "I'll ask the concierge what's good in these parts."

"Good idea," Decker said. "We can't leave just yet though."

"Why not?" Colum asked, perplexed.

"I'm waiting for someone," Decker replied. "An old friend."

"Now who would you know in London?" Colum narrowed his eyes. "I can't imagine you've been here before."

"You're correct. I've never visited the United Kingdom until now. That doesn't alter the fact that a friend is meeting me here." Decker glanced at his phone. "She should have been here five minutes ago."

"She?" Colum observed Decker. "You're meeting a woman?"

"Indeed, I am." Decker glanced toward the hotel bar's double doors as they swung open and a familiar figure stepped into the room. "And here she is."

Colum followed Decker's gaze, his eyes settling on an attractive young woman with shoulder-length blonde hair. She wore a black leather jacket and tight jeans. "That's the person your meeting?"

"It is," Decker said as she walked toward them, a warm smile breaking out on her face. "Colum O'Shea, I'd like you to meet Mina Parkinson."

# NINE

THE BASEMENT ROOM at the University of Central London might have passed for a storage area, and it did indeed contain countless shelves packed with books, old research papers, and boxes stuffed with items that had wound up under the Criminology Department's stewardship, many of them related to decades, or even centuries old crimes. There were the bones of a murder victim discovered under the floor of a seventeenth century cottage, the skull cleaved by a long-lost weapon. An antique seltzer bottle used by a Victorian era duchess to poison her husband. A silver cigarette case with a bullet hole in it. These and hundreds of other items languished in the dark and cramped chamber, forgotten by all except the few researchers who occasionally removed an item for study.

Today there was only one person occupying the room. Historical Criminologist, Callie Balfour, sat hunched over Jack the Ripper's knife, retrieved from the townhouse in Mayfair, and examined the blade with a desk mounted magnifying glass. The dark stains on the old metal were blood, she was sure of it. A testament to the violence this weapon had inflicted over a century before. She turned the knife over with a gloved hand and sat back in her chair, staring at it. She wondered how many people had felt its cold bite against their neck. The last thing they would ever feel. There were the canonical five, to be sure, but how many other victims had this knife claimed? More to the point, why had it even been there? Someone had gone to a lot of trouble to make sure the person bricked up in that small underground room never committed another act of violence. They had been content to let one of the most notorious serial killers of the nineteenth century remain anonymous. But why? Surely it would have served the public interest better to unmask the maniac, bring him to trial, and put an end to the terror gripping the streets of Whitechapel.

She yawned. Callie had barely slept since the cellar chamber's discovery. At first she ran on excitement and adrenaline, barely able to tear her eyes from the fascinating artifacts they had removed. There were newspaper cuttings collected by Jack himself, a gruesomely narcissistic homage to his deadly work. There was the map of Whitechapel with faded markings showing the scene of each crime. Some of these related to known Ripper victims. A few matched murders tentatively attributed to the killer, but never included in the official count. These, Callie noted, would swell the tally of Jack's confirmed victims. Most chilling of all were the marks that did not relate to any known murder. At least eight of them. Did these faded dots on the map represent slayings never investigated? Victorian London, and the East End slums in particular, were a harsh, violent place. It would have been easy to cover up a misdeed when those against whom the crime was committed were held in such scant regard by the authorities of the time. The destitute. Prostitutes. Petty criminals and pickpockets. Alcoholics. The long-term unemployed. These were the forgotten people of the capital, a blight on the sensibilities of the gentry. It was easier to look the other way rather than confront the ugliness of a class system that so readily highlighted the unequal distribution of wealth across the city.

Later, once the exhilaration had worn off, Callie found herself lost in morbid fascination. Even when she tried to rest, her mind refused to shut off. She felt like a runaway train hurtling toward an unknown destination with no ability to stop.

Then there was the missing body. The source of much consternation over the past forty-eight hours. How could someone have stolen it? The news hadn't even broken regarding the discovery yet. That would not happen until the next morning when someone placed an anonymous tip to the London newspapers. When she thought about the missing corpse, she felt a flash of anger. Imagine what interesting finds lay in wait upon that body. What was in his pockets? How had he died? Most frustrating of all, for the first time in over a century, they would've been able to look upon the true face of a monster. Instead, they were left with nothing.

"I wasn't expecting to find anyone still down here. It's gone eight o'clock."

A voice drifted through Callie's musings, shattering her train of thought. She looked up to see Martin Slade, a graduate assistant with the criminology department, and one of the two other university personnel who had been present during the initial examination of the cellar room, standing in the doorway.

"It's hard to tear myself away." Callie knew she should go home, have some dinner, and crawl into bed. Get an early night. A sleeping pill or two would do the trick. Tomorrow she would wake up refreshed and ready to go.

"Find anything new?" Martin approached the desk and sank into a chair opposite Callie.

"Not much." Callie glanced toward the knife. "I've taken samples of the material on the blade and sent them out for analysis, although I'm pretty sure it will be blood."

"Just think of all the people who died because of that thing." Martin's gaze flicked downward. "It's hard not to look at it."

"I think it's horrific." Callie rubbed her eyes. "Fascinating, but still creepy."

"What about the body?" Martin drew his eyes from the blade. "Have you heard anything about that?"

"Nothing useful." Callie had phoned the police for an update earlier in the day. She hoped they would have good news. There was none. It was like the body had vanished in a puff of smoke. Not that the disappearance of a half-mummified corpse ranked high on the local constabulary's list of must solve cases, even if it was of historical importance. They had other concerns. Like the brutal murder of a college student on her way back home from an evening in the pub with friends. A killing that had occurred on the same night and within a block of the Ripper's former home. A crime similar in method to Jack's own atrocities. The chilling coincidence was not lost on her.

"They'll find him, you'll see."

"I hope so." Callie wished she shared her colleague's optimism. She yawned again, exhaustion forcing its way to the surface. "I'm going home. You should too."

"In a while. I want to take another look at those newspaper clippings." Martin nodded toward the cuttings removed from the cellar wall, now in a box separated by sheets of archival quality cardboard.

"Be careful," Callie warned. "I haven't made copies yet."

"Naturally." Martin nodded.

Callie pushed her chair back and stood up. She picked up her purse and turned toward the door, before looking back at Martin. "Lock up when you leave. I don't want anything else to go missing."

"I'll take care of it." Martin's mouth creased into a thin smile. "I'll see you tomorrow."

"Tomorrow." Callie reached the door, then hesitated, overcome by a sudden sense of unease. She glanced back at Martin, who hadn't moved. She tried to fathom where the strange feeling had come from, but couldn't, so she shrugged it off and headed for the stairs.

# TEN

"I CAN'T BELIEVE you're in London," Mina said when she arrived at the table occupied by Decker and Colum. A happy grin lit up her face. She wrapped her arms around Decker and didn't let go until he gently extricated himself.

"It's good to see you too," Decker replied. Mina had changed since they parted ways in Shackleton, Alaska, the previous year. Her hair was shorter and flowed in a cascade of lustrous blonde to her shoulders. The glasses were gone too, no doubt replaced by contacts. She looked confident and self-assured, a cosmopolitan young woman in the big city. "You look fantastic. All grown up."

"Thank you," Mina replied, a slight blush tinging her cheeks. "You're looking pretty good yourself, mister monster hunter."

Colum sat with his arms folded, a bemused expression on his face. "If the two of you are done fawning over each other…"

"Your choice of sidekick has gone downhill since we parted ways," Mina said, eyeing Colum.

"I'm not his sidekick." Colum tried to look annoyed but could not hide his amusement. "If anything, he's mine."

"Really?" Decker chuckled, casting a quick look Colum's way. "Is that why I had to save you from Grendel when we were in the caves under Astrid's house?"

"That's not how I remember it."

"The sling you're wearing would beg to differ," Mina said.

"Actually, it proves just the opposite," Colum replied, nodding toward Decker. "I was saving his ass when I got injured."

"You keep telling yourself that." Decker laughed.

"I will." Colum looked longingly toward his empty pint glass. He pushed his chair back and stood up. "If we're having a reunion, I'm getting another drink. It'll stave off the hunger."

"I'll take a pint too, if you're going up to the bar," Mina said as Colum stepped away from the table. "A lager will be nice."

"One round of drinks coming up," Colum said. As he departed, he gave Mina an appreciative look, his eyes lingering.

Mina met his gaze with a flirtatious smile, then turned her attention to Decker. "Grendel, huh?"

"You're not to repeat that." Decker chided himself for his inadvertent slip. He wasn't used to the level of secrecy that CUSP demanded and would hear about it from Colum later, he was sure. "Forget I said anything at all."

"My lips are sealed," Mina said, even though the look on her face suggested she was burning with curiosity. "I guess you're working for Adam Hunt, then?"

"Again, not at liberty to divulge."

"Right." Mina flicked a strand of hair from her forehead. "You know, not answering is as good as saying yes."

"How's college life treating you?" Decker asked, changing the subject.

"How do you think life's treating me?" Mina said. "I'm in England, of all places, studying at the University of Central London for an entire year. I never thought I'd get out of Shackleton, let alone this. It's freaking amazing."

"You deserve it." Decker motioned for Mina to sit and then retook his own seat.

"I know. Although I suspect my college applications received a little help. I got offers from three universities. All of them first tier."

"Anything you did, you achieved all on your own," Decker said. "Besides, it's one thing to get into college, it's another thing to excel there."

"Been keeping tabs on me, huh?"

"Only through the emails we've exchanged."

"Sure," Mina said. "It's okay if you have. I kind of like knowing that you're out there, watching over me. It makes me feel safe."

Decker smiled noncommittally.

Mina unzipped her jacket and slipped it off, then hung it on the back of the chair. Underneath, she wore a white tee with the words *don't sweat it* printed in bold black lettering. "So, what brings you to London? Let me guess. Jack the Ripper?"

"Again..."

"Of course. Not at liberty to say." Mina shook her head. "I'm not sure I like the new, secretive John Decker."

"Comes with the job."

"I get that," Mina said. "But it's me you're talking to, not some random shmuck. I've kept quiet about what happened in Shackleton, haven't I? That practically makes me one of Adam Hunt's inner circle."

"I'm not so sure about that." Decker looked up as Colum returned holding three pints of beer that he'd avoided spilling a single drop of despite the sling which rendered one arm practically immobile.

"There you go," he said, depositing a drink in front of Mina. He handed the second one to Decker and kept the third for himself, retaking his seat. "What are we talking about?"

"Jack the Ripper," Mina blurted before Decker could speak. "John was telling me why you're in London."

"He shouldn't have said anything about that." Colum shot Decker an accusatory look.

"I knew it." Mina flashed a smug grin. "He's not dead, is he? That murder the other night, the girl who got her throat slashed, that was him, wasn't it?"

"Good going, genius," Decker said to Colum. "A twenty-year-old girl just outsmarted you. I had mentioned nothing about Jack the Ripper."

"I'm almost twenty one," Mina protested. "And you shouldn't blame your sidekick just because I outwitted him. It was hardly a fair fight."

"For the second time, I'm not his sidekick. And you didn't outsmart me," Colum said, scowling. "I also paid for your drink; I might remind you."

"That you shouldn't have," Decker said to Mina. "You're not twenty-one yet."

"I don't need to be," Mina replied. "The legal drinking age in England is eighteen."

"She's right," Colum said, coming to her defense.

"Thank you." Mina took a sip of her drink, then turned her attention to Decker. "Tell me about Jack the Ripper. Do you have any leads yet? I bet you do."

"That's not your concern," Colum said.

"I can help." Mina's eyes were wide with enthusiasm.

"I doubt it." Colum shook his head. "I think we have it covered."

"Really?" Mina leaned forward and looked between the two men. "Have you tried to get into that cellar where they imprisoned Jack to look for clues?"

"No. I'm not saying it wouldn't be useful, but I'd rather not alert the authorities to our presence if I can help it."

"We work better under the radar," Decker said. "Besides, the powers that be will never believe that Jack the Ripper is still alive and running around."

"That's not a bad thing," Colum added. "Cuts down on the red tape when we capture him."

"I can help you get in there," Mina said. "You won't draw any unwanted attention, I promise."

"If this is your way of muscling in on the case, it won't work." Colum folded his arms. "I've read the report regarding what happened in Shackleton and I'm aware of your role in its resolution, but you're still a civilian."

"Okay, then." Mina sat back in her chair and picked up her drink. She took a sip and remained silent for a few moments before speaking again. "But I know where all the artifacts recovered from that room went, including the Ripper's knife and the map he used it to keep track of his murder victims. I'm also a friend of the one person who can get you into Jack's lair on the down low. But if you don't want my help, that's fine."

If this impressed Colum, he didn't show it. "Why don't you tell me who your contact is, and we'll check it out. Then, if what you're saying is true…"

"Nice try." Mina laughed. "You won't fool me that easily. If you agree that I can help catch the Ripper, I'll take you to my friend. She will be a huge help, you'll see. What do you say?"

"Looks like you've been outmaneuvered a second time in as many minutes," Decker said to Colum. "We might as well agree to her demands. Mina is quite tenacious, and very smart. Besides, I'd love to get a look inside that room."

"Very well then." Colum didn't look pleased at this turn of events. "But only if she really can get us into Jack's den, and only if Adam agrees."

"Yay." Mina was bursting with excitement. "I can't believe I'm going to hunt down Jack the Ripper. This is so cool."

"Don't get too excited," Decker cautioned. "Even if Adam Hunt agrees, you will help from the sidelines, nothing more. I will not put you in danger again."

"I love how you look out for me. You're like the dad I never had." Mina's eyes twinkled as she looked at Decker. "I can't wait. The two of us catching a monster together. It will be just like old times."

# ELEVEN

DETECTIVE INSPECTOR ELLIOT Mead of the Metropolitan police's Homicide and Serious Crime Command should have gone straight home at the end of his shift, but he didn't. Instead, he went to the King's Head pub. This wasn't his intended destination when he left the station, but the murder in the alley of Hay's Mews had been playing on his mind for two days and he just ended up there. A detour steered by his subconscious.

They were no closer to finding the killer than in the first hours after the crime. Uniformed officers had canvassed the entire area around Hay's Mews the previous day, including the pub that sat on the corner. They had turned up nothing. The only lead so far was a CCTV camera further down the street that had caught a near collision when a pedestrian wandered into the road in front of an SUV. The camera's image was good enough to show the incident, but too grainy to reveal much else. The figure was nothing more than a dark and blurry shape, and they had failed to track down the vehicle. With the number of SUVs in the city, they might as well not even bother looking. To add to their problems, the camera only recorded in black and white, so they couldn't discern the SUV's color. Even the weird coincidence of another crime which had occurred close by at around the same time had produced no viable information. Earlier that day a construction crew had found a body believed to be that of Jack the Ripper walled up in an underground room on the Mews. A body that had subsequently disappeared, stolen from under the nose of the ambulance crew tasked with removing it. While the ambulance driver remembered seeing the SUV avoid what she assumed was a drunk exiting the pub, she could provide no more details than the CCTV camera. And despite the strange coincidence, Elliott could see no plausible connection between the missing body and the murder in the alley.

So now he sat at the bar in the Kings Head and nursed a pint of lager, hoping he would overhear something useful. The victim had a blood-alcohol level of 0.06, which meant she had consumed several drinks prior to her demise. The King's Head was the closest pub and therefore it made sense that she had purchased at least one drink here prior to entering the alleyway across the street. Earlier in the evening she had met with friends for dinner. At the meal's conclusion, she turned down the offer of a ride home and told them she wanted to walk instead. She left alone and had no other plans they were aware of. Maybe she met someone else after saying goodbye to her friends. A background check had revealed she did not have a romantic partner, and cell phone records showed she had placed no calls. She probably stopped into the Kings Head for a top up. Another drink to keep the buzz going. Was it possible she attracted her killer's attention while in this very pub? Elliott felt a pang of sorrow. If only she had gotten in the car with her friends, she would still be alive.

But she wasn't.

And it was his job to find the person responsible. He wasn't getting anywhere here, though. Not tonight. There was a band playing, the music loud and brash, good only for drowning out the lead singer's off-key wailing. Even if someone let something slip, he wouldn't hear it over the cacophony of noise coming from the small stage at the rear of the room. He would be better off going home to his wife and daughter and trying to put the grisly details of the life snuffed out across the road from his mind. At least until morning. Elliott finished his drink, slipped off the barstool, and left the pub.

# TWELVE

ADAM HUNT AGREED to Mina's demands, albeit reluctantly. She was, he grumbled over the phone, a pain in the ass, if a useful one. Besides, she already knew more about CUSP than he would have liked and had at least proven that she could keep her mouth shut. Given her prior knowledge, and the fact that she had already tricked Colum into revealing their current mission, he couldn't see the point in arguing with her. Decker suspected there was another reason, too. Once Mina finished her education, it was likely she would be offered a position in CUSP, anyway. The organization preferred to bring people into the fold rather than be forced to deal with civilians who possessed knowledge they should not have. This was partly how Decker himself had ended up working for Adam Hunt, who had spent a good deal of time in Alaska obfuscating rather than helping. It was only after it became obvious deception would not work that Hunt changed his mind. Not that CUSP took all and sundry. There were, Decker suspected, other ways of dealing with those who did not rise to the organization's rigorous standards. What those methods were, he didn't know, and he wasn't sure he wanted to.

Regardless of whether Hunt was happy with the situation, it amounted to the same thing. Mina was now a part of the team, at least for as long as they were in London. The only caveat, insisted upon by Decker despite her protestations, was that she would not be put in harm's way. With that agreed-upon, Mina got to work right away, and offered to show them the site of the recent murder.

It was dark by the time they left the hotel and made the short walk to Hays Mews. As they walked, Mina pointed out the three-story townhouse where the Ripper's den had been discovered. The building was locked up and empty, with no hint of light showing through the windows. They moved on quickly. Mina had promised to get them inside through official channels and Decker was content to wait, at least for now.

A little way past the townhouse, on the other side of the road, was the alleyway within which the murder had occurred. A lone uniformed officer stood guard in front of a ribbon of blue and white crime scene tape strung across the alley's entrance.

Decker paused and took in his surroundings. A pub stood on the corner. A live band was performing. The heavy thud of a bass beat spoiled the peace. A few groups of patrons huddled around tables arranged on the curb outside, braving the chilly British evening with thick coats while they drank and joked among themselves.

No one paid Decker and his companions any heed.

"Shall we take a peek?" Colum asked.

"How are we going to do that?" Decker asked, nodding toward the cop standing at the alley's entrance.

"Leave it to me." Colum started across the road. He reached into his coat pocket and removed a leather wallet that he flipped open as he approached the police officer.

The young man straightened as Colum drew near. "This area is off limits, sir."

"Detective Chief Inspector Clarkson, with Major Investigations," Colum said, flashing the contents of the wallet, then snapping it quickly shut. He nodded back toward Decker and Mina. "These two are with me. Specialists. I need to show them the scene."

The young police officer hesitated, then nodded, apparently

deciding that confirming his superior's identity would cast him in a poor light. "Go ahead, sir."

"Thank you." Colum ducked under the tape and waited for the others.

As Mina reached the cordon, she smiled at the police officer. "What's your name?"

"Constable Burton, ma'am."

"Well, keep up the excellent work, Constable Burton." She lifted the tape and stepped under, striding past the two men toward the crime scene.

Colum glanced at Decker as they followed behind. "She's not a shy one, is she?"

"She's on her best behavior right now." Decker replied.

"Lord help us."

"Speaking of good behavior, what was all that back there?"

"What?"

"Flashing ID. Telling that cop you were a detective?"

"The warrant card?" Colum said. "I've had it for a few years. Helps to open doors."

"It's also illegal," Decker replied. "What if he'd checked your credentials?"

"He wouldn't. Trust me." Colum said.

"You could have gotten us all arrested."

"But I didn't," Colum replied. "I know what I'm doing."

"Just tell me ahead of time before you impersonate any more police officers," Decker said.

"I'll do my best."

"Good." They had caught up with Mina now. She had stopped at the spot of the attack. "Make sure not to touch anything," Decker warned her.

"I know," she replied. "I watched a lot of police procedurals back in Shackleton. There wasn't much else to do until you came along."

"I'm flattered." Decker kneeled and examined the pool of blood that had dried on the concrete alley floor. Then he stood and studied the marks on the walls. "The victim was assaulted from behind, her throat cut before she knew what was happening. She never even put up a struggle."

"How on earth would you know that?" Colum asked.

"Look at the blood spatter on the walls," Decker replied, pointing toward the dried blood on the brickwork. "The initial attack caused that. The killer put his arm around her neck from behind and drew the knife across her throat. Now look at the alley floor. She bled out in the same spot, collapsing before she succumbed to her injuries. If she were aware of her situation, she would have been fleeing, so forward momentum alone would have carried her beyond the spot of the initial encounter, if only for a few feet."

"Maybe he restrained her so she couldn't flee," Colum said.

"Possibly," Decker admitted. "But the blood on the wall is in a tight pattern, which makes it unlikely that she was struggling. Not that it matters. The more interesting thing is how close we are to the building where they found the Ripper. The timing of the crime, and the location, confirm what we already suspect. Jack is our killer. But it also tells us something else."

"And that would be?" Colum asked.

"He was desperate to kill," Mina said before Decker could answer. "It was more important to him than anything else."

"Precisely." Decker nodded. "We know he needs blood in order to extend his life. But we also know he was out of action for a hundred and thirty years. An hour or two longer would have made little difference. It would have been safer to move further afield, yet he committed a murder within earshot of the very place he had just escaped. Instead of fleeing, he was looking for a victim."

"Maybe he thought a quick kill would aid his escape," Colum said. "Provide him with renewed energy."

"Maybe." Decker looked thoughtful. "Either way, he will probably kill again."

"Unless we stop him first," Colum said.

"Yes. Unless we do that." Decker glanced around. The music coming from the pub had stopped now. The band was on a break.

"There's not much else we'll find out here. I don't know about you guys, but I could do with something to eat."

"Now you're talking," Colum said, his face brightening.

"There's a great curry house near here, and they're open late," Mina said. "How about that?"

"I love curry," Colum said. "Food of the Gods."

"Sure, why not? We can catch up some more." Decker smiled. He gestured to Mina. "After you."

Mina started back down the alley and ducked under the crime scene tape. The cop gave her a cursory glance, then turned away.

Colum and Decker followed behind. The Irishman nodded toward the officer and thanked him. Then they continued down the street. As they walked, Colum eyed Mina appreciatively.

"Don't even think about it," Decker said, keeping his voice low.

"What?" Colum tried to look innocent.

"You know very well," Decker replied. "She's too young, and you're not her type."

"And how would you know what her type is?"

"I don't," Decker said, his face stony. "But regardless, you aren't it. Understand?"

"Yeah." Colum dug his hands into his pockets. "I understand well enough, dad."

They had reached the corner now. Mina was still several steps ahead. She looked back over her shoulder, oblivious to their hushed conversation. "Would you pair hurry? I'm hungry."

# THIRTEEN

ZOE GARRITY LEFT her boyfriend's bedsit on Dean Road a little after ten in the evening and walked back toward the university campus. She had an early class the next day and didn't want to be out late, despite Jason's request that she stay the night. She was thinking of dumping him, anyway. He was boorish and immature. Hardly long-term relationship material. She wasn't even sure why she started seeing him. Maybe it was the Honda motorcycle that enhanced his bad boy image, or his cavalier attitude that oozed confidence. Except now she saw through him. The bike was a pile of junk that should've been on the scrapheap years ago, and his self-assured demeanor nothing more than a cloak that hid a spiteful and mean temperament, no doubt fueled by his own insecurities.

He was, in short, a jackass.

Zoe would be better off without him and had almost said as much that very night. The only thing that stopped her was a nagging conviction that he would not take the news well. Having seen him fly into a rage before, she had no desire to antagonize him at that moment. She would wait and do it in public. Or better yet, send a text message. It was hard to abuse a phone.

Still, there was one thing she regretted. Not allowing him to walk her back to campus. The streets were unusually empty, the moonless night made all the gloomier by thick cloud cover and a steady drizzle of rain. His presence would have put her at ease, even though she suspected he only offered in the hope she would allow him to crash at her place, and not through genuine concern about her walking the streets alone at night.

She picked up the pace. It would take another twenty minutes to reach the flat she shared with two other students in a block of university accommodation, a stone's throw from the school's administration building. At times like this Zoe wished she could afford a car, but even if money were no object, she probably would not own one. Space was at a premium in the city, and the university did not provide parking spots for its students. Instead, she relied on a bicycle to get around, and she hadn't even taken that. It had been a nice evening, and she wanted to enjoy the last vestiges of summer weather before autumn hit full stride and the temperatures plummeted.

Now though, she fought back a tingle of apprehension and wished she were already back at the flat, safe in her bedroom. She had made this walk dozens of times, but tonight it felt different. Maybe it was the persistent drizzle that had kept everyone indoors, or maybe it was the recent unsolved murder of another lone student walking home in the dark.

"Get a grip, Zoe," she chided herself, hoping that the sound of her own voice would break the sense of unease. And it did, if only for a moment. But then the disquietude returned, filling the silence with an unspoken dread.

It would, she decided, be in her best interest to reach her destination as quickly as possible. There was a shortcut up ahead. Ambry Lane. A narrow footpath that cut between two office buildings and a football field sized piece of derelict land waiting for redevelopment before depositing her on Frogmore Street. She didn't like the shortcut at the best of times, but it shaved almost six minutes off her walk. That made it worth considering. By the time she reached the narrow alleyway that marked the beginning of the lane, Zoe had decided what to do. Without giving herself a chance to change her mind, she took a left turn and stepped into the alley.

It was even darker once Zoe was off the street. The alleyway stretched ahead, swathed in darkness. Only a thin break between the buildings, several hundred feet away, provided a point of reference that told her where the alley ended, and the scrubland began.

She forged ahead, eager to be out of the claustrophobic space created by the buildings that pressed in on both sides. She kept her eyes forward, concentrating on the widening gap that signaled an escape from the alley's confinement.

At least, until she heard a light footstep behind her.

Zoe's breath caught in her throat. She glanced over her shoulder. She saw nothing at first. But then, as her eyes adjusted, she noticed a shape silhouetted against the the alley's entrance.

Someone was behind her.

Zoe resisted the urge to run. For all she knew, this was just an innocent pedestrian taking the same shortcut she was. It might even be another student at her college. The campus began a little way down Frogmore street, on the other side of the empty scrubland. There was no need to panic. Except she couldn't help herself. The unease that had plagued her since leaving Jason's bedsit had turned into a screeching alarm. She wished she hadn't taken the shortcut. But it was too late now. Even if she wanted to, she couldn't go back, not with that figure blocking the way.

She took a deep breath and forced herself to keep going, her walk turning into a trot. She would soon emerge from between the buildings. Then she would have to traverse the derelict plot of land and follow a short access road before reaching Frogmore Street. It wasn't ideal, but what choice did she have?

Except that the footsteps were louder now. Whoever was behind her was drawing closer. She didn't dare risk another glance backwards. She was too afraid. Instead, she quickened her pace, desperate to be out of the alley. Then, when she was only a few steps away from the scrubland, she sensed someone right behind her, much too close.

Zoe flinched and turned, a scream on her lips.

The figure kept going, unperturbed, pushing past and bumping her shoulder.

"Sorry," a male voice said.

Then the figure was moving off down the path and onto the scrubland, leaving only a faint odor of alcohol as he went. Just a young man on his way home from the pub.

Zoe's heart was racing. She watched him go, overcome with relief. She leaned against the wall and almost laughed out loud. Another moment and she would've been screaming bloody murder. She stayed there for a minute, calming her frazzled nerves, and watched the man make his way through the empty plot of land and arrive at the access road on the other side.

Finally, when she had composed herself, Zoe started off, following in the young man's footsteps. She emerged from the alleyway, relieved to be out in the open, and lowered her head against the rain, which was coming down harder now. She had made it halfway across the derelict plot when her nervousness returned.

She stopped and looked around. What triggered this fresh bout of unease? The undeveloped plot of land was bordered on all four sides by buildings, uneven rectangles of flat blackness against the dark sky. To her left the land rose into a small hill choked with weeds, the result of the earth being flattened ready for whatever building had been planned for this spot. A backhoe stood idle near the mound, its bucket resting on the earth as if it had grown tired of all the heavy lifting and slouched down. Here and there, she picked out other shapes she could not identify, probably debris left over from the demolition of the original building.

Except one.

This shape was moving. It extricated itself from the blackness near the digger and started toward her.

Zoe stood rooted to the spot, frozen with fear. There had been someone else here all along, watching from the shadows. Waiting. This time, she knew it would not be another student returning to campus, or a patron stumbling home from a night of boozing.

Now she found her feet.

Zoe turned and ran.

Behind her, the figure in the shadows did the same. She could hear him giving chase, his footfalls heavy.

She risked a quick glance over her shoulder and let out a sob of dismay. He was faster than her, closing the gap between them. She looked forward again, focused on the access road. If she could get to it, he might give up. There were blocks of flats on Frogmore Street. People. She could see the glow from the windows of buildings beyond the scrubland. Safety was only a short distance away.

She might make it.

Hope rose up within her, battling against the fear. A few more steps, that was all it would take. But then, just as she reached the access road, she felt a hand grip her coat collar.

She cried out and twisted, desperate to escape, but it was no good. She was being dragged back into the wasteland even as she struggled to break free. She opened her mouth to scream. Maybe someone in those flats on Frogmore Street would hear the disturbance and come to her aid. But before she could make a sound, Zoe felt a touch of steel to her neck, cold and sharp, slicing deep into the soft flesh under her chin, penetrating to the bone. And as the life pumped from her severed arteries, Zoe felt one last thing. Her killer's quickening breath hot on her skin as he leaned close to savor the moment of death…

# FOURTEEN

ABRAHAM PROWLED THE DARK STREETS. He had no idea where he was going, he only knew that he did not want to return to the decrepit, abandoned building in Bethnal Green. He'd spent two days hiding out there before finally mustering the energy to move. The unfortunate rats that had become his meals over that time had provided meager sustenance, and he was still no closer to finding the one thing that would prolong his life and rejuvenate his appearance. The fob watch. Without it he could survive for a time, but it was only through the watch that he would be saved. The blood of his victims, alone, was not enough. This much had been proven. The watch was still out there. He could feel it calling out to him. But the connection was weak. Abraham suspected this was because of Abberline and his companion. They were shielding the watch from Abraham, even from beyond the grave. How they had accomplished this he could not fathom, but there would be time to find out. There were more pressing concerns right now. Like finding a meal that didn't require catching a rat. This was an easier problem to resolve. There was a fish and chip shop up ahead, the warm light from its windows spilling across the pavement.

Abraham approached with a measure of trepidation. The street was empty, but the chance he would be seen increased the closer he got to the shop. There might be customers there, people who would remember a disfigured and wretched face such as his. Not to mention his clothing, outdated and filthy, practically falling apart. He could not afford to attract attention. But he need not have worried. The chip shop was empty, a closed sign hanging in the window. There was no one around except for a lone figure behind the counter, busy cleaning up after the night's service.

Abraham watched the chippie's owner going about his business. A faint odor of fried food hung in the air, a testament to the nourishment that lay just out of reach beyond the glass. He considered banging on the window, drawing the man's attention. Maybe he could scrounge a handful of leftovers. But that would be pointless, he knew. It was more likely that the owner, terrified by Abraham's appearance, would call the police. Even so, he stood there a moment longer staring wistfully towards the counter. And perhaps he lingered a little too long because the shop's owner looked his way, as if sensing he was the subject of Abraham's gaze. But instead of fear, the man's face creased into a mask of disgust.

"Get away from here," he shouted toward Abraham, waving his hand in a shooing motion for emphasis. "Go find another doorway to sleep in, why don't you. Useless F'ing vagrant."

Abraham didn't move.

"What the…" Now the man's expression had turned to anger. "Didn't you hear me? Get out of here before I call the old bill."

Abraham glared at him through the window. Any thought of slinking away into the night was abandoned. He wasn't going to let this man demean him. Threaten him. It was time Abraham took what he wanted. He turned away from the window, made his way back down the street and around the corner. The store owner thought he'd taken care of the problem, no doubt. Abraham knew better. There was another road running behind the row of shops, narrow and dark. Wheelie bins stood next to the rear doors of several units, alongside empty pallets stacked in haphazard piles, and a bundle of cardboard boxes, broken apart and heaped on top of each other.

Abraham made his way down the service road until he found the right door, easily identified by the name stenciled upon it. *White Swan Chip Shop*. He lingered in the shadows near the door, biding his time. He didn't have to wait long.

The shop's owner emerged carrying a white bucket. He stepped across the road to a sewer grate and tipped the bucket, depositing gallons of spent cooking oil into the drain. He turned back toward the shop, a cigarette hanging from one side of his mouth.

Abraham stepped out of the gloom and blocked the door.

The shop owner froze. A look of panic crossed his face. He released the bucket, letting it clatter to the ground where it rolled away and came to rest near the pile of spent pallets. "What you want?" he asked, his voice cracking. "I've already called the police, just so you know."

Abraham took a step forward into a pool of light cast by a lamp fixed to the wall above the door. He reached down, his hand finding the knife in what remained of his trouser pocket.

"Sweet Jesus." The shopkeeper's eyes flew wide with panic as he looked upon Abraham's ghastly countenance. "What in God's name are you?"

Abraham didn't reply. He wasn't sure he could trust himself to form a coherent word yet. But even if he could, he wouldn't have said anything. There was no point when his corpse-like appearance alone elicited such abject terror.

The shopkeeper glanced left, then right, seeking a viable means of escape, desperate to flee the nightmarish figure that now advanced upon him.

Abraham took another step, closing the gap between them and ensuring his victim had nowhere to run.

The shopkeeper's eyes flicked down to the knife. "Please don't," he said, each word freighted with panic. "For the love of God, let me be."

Abraham had no intention of letting him be, or even letting him live. He watched the man for a second more, savoring his anguish, then lunged forward, bringing the knife up in a swift and fluid motion.

The shopkeeper let out a terrified yelp moments before the blade intersected his throat. He stood in disbelief, hands clutched to his throat, trying desperately to staunch the flow of blood. But it was no use. As the life pumped through his fingers, the shopkeeper tumbled backwards, his head smacking into the concrete next to the drain with a sickening thud.

Abraham watched the man fade away, his blood running crimson into the drain and mixing with the cooking oil that had preceded it. Then, when the shop owner was nothing more than a lifeless carcass, Abraham gripped him by the hair and dragged him back into the shop, slamming the door behind them.

# FIFTEEN

THERE WAS ONLY one other table occupied when Decker, Colum, and Mina arrived at the curry house. A swarthy gentleman with a sagging gut that hung over his pants told them to take a seat anywhere. He didn't seem at all perturbed by new customers so late in the evening. This was in stark contrast to Decker's time in Wolf Haven, where everything was closed and dark by nine o'clock at night. The ability to find food at all hours was a luxury he'd missed since leaving New York City, where many eating establishments operated around the clock. During his years as a homicide detective, he'd grown used to dining at odd hours and he felt a nostalgic comfort in the pursuit of food at such a late hour.

As they ate, Decker caught up with all that had happened in Mina's life since they last saw each other. They had kept in touch sporadically since Shackleton, but now she gushed about college and the wonderful opportunities afforded her. Such as the move to London, facilitated via an exchange program that allowed the brightest students to study abroad for a year. She beamed with contentment.

Afterward, when the meal was finished, they parted ways. Mina promised she would be in touch as soon as she could arrange access to Jack's cellar room. Then she climbed into a taxi at Decker's insistence, despite her protests that public transport was safe enough. He didn't want her on the streets alone. Not with Jack on the loose.

After she'd gone, Colum and Decker strolled back to the hotel. After they entered the lobby Colum paused.

"You fancy a nightcap?"

"I don't think so." It was heading toward midnight and Decker wanted to be fresh and with a clear head the next day. He stepped toward the elevator. "But you go ahead."

"Nah. I'm not so much into drinking on my own." Colum followed Decker across the lobby. "I'm not sure I'm ready for bed yet, though. I think I'll look online, see if I can find out who owned that townhouse back in the 1800s."

"Good luck with that," Decker said as the elevator arrived. They rode up to the eighth floor and went their separate ways. Upon reaching his hotel room door, Decker turned back to Colum. "Don't stay up too late. I want you wide-awake tomorrow."

"You realize I'm the senior agent here, right?" Colum said. "You're still a rookie."

"When it comes to monsters, you're the rookie." Decker placed his key card over the reader and waited for the click as the bolt drew back before opening his door. "Grendel was your first, I believe."

"It's quality that counts, not quantity." Colum couldn't help smiling as he pushed open his own door and stepped inside. "See you in the morning. Sleep tight."

Decker nodded and entered his room. He closed the door and engaged the security latch, then hung his coat in the closet. Beyond the hotel room window stretched the open expanse of Hyde Park, and beyond this, a million lights twinkling all across the city.

Decker stood at the window and gazed toward the crowded skyline. Somewhere out there, amid those burning points of light, a killer prowled. A man who should have been dead and buried more than a century ago. Instead, he'd been freed to cut a bloody swath through the streets. A cunning animal fueled by the need for blood. He would kill again, Decker was sure. The only question was, when?

He turned away from the window and perched on the edge of the bed, then took his phone out, placing a call to Nancy. As he waited for her to answer a sense of foreboding enveloped him. He hung up and typed a quick text to Mina, relieved when she sent a reply right back. She had reached the halls of residence and was already in bed. Satisfied that she was all right, he called Nancy again. Yet even when she answered, her voice full of excitement to hear from him, he could not shake the feeling of unease. Mina was safe for now. He only hoped he could keep it that way.

# SIXTEEN

THE FIRST THING Abraham did was check the premises to make sure no one else was there. He left the chip shop's owner laying in the back storage room, near the rear door, and headed for the front of the shop. After satisfying himself that the ground floor was empty, he returned to the storeroom and mounted a set of stairs to the second floor.

The upper level turned out to be a small apartment with a living room, bedroom, and bathroom. The chip shop owner lived on the premises. And he lived alone. Just like the floor below, there was no one here except Abraham. There was also no sign the shop owner was cohabiting. One toothbrush in the bathroom. A single TV tray in the living room with an unwashed plate sitting on it, the remnants of a meal clearly visible. A narrow bed wide enough for one person occupied the bedroom, crumpled sheets denoting that whoever had last occupied it, presumably the dead man downstairs, had not bothered to make it. He also hadn't washed the sheets in a while, judging by the head shaped sweat stain on the pillowcase.

Abraham didn't care about any of this. The man he'd recently dispatched might be a slob, but the suite of rooms was pure luxury compared to where Abraham had spent the last two nights.

Satisfied that no one would disturb him, he made his way back downstairs. He looked down at the body lying on the floor in a widening pool of blood. It would do no good to leave it here, and he was loath to dispose of it elsewhere. If found it would lead the authorities to the shop. Abraham had set out to find a meal and instead stumbled upon a place to lay his head too. He would not squander this good fortune by risking discovery of the chip shop owner's body.

He glanced around, looking for a suitable place to stash the corpse, and in doing so his eyes fell upon a smaller room occupying one quarter of the storage area's floor space. Constructed of metal, it boasted a thick door secured by a hefty latch. A blast of sub-zero air escaped when he opened the door. This was some kind of cold storage room, and it was freezing inside. Shelves lined three walls, laden with food. There was enough to feed a small army. If Abraham possessed the capability, he would have grinned. Instead, he returned to the outer room and grabbed the corpse by the hair once again, dragging it into the cold storage room. He retreated and closed the door, latching it. Stepping past the trail of blood smeared across the floor, he went to the front of the shop and found a pair of battered deep-fried sausages sitting under a heat lamp inside a glass display case on the counter. These he consumed with gusto, before turning his attention to the chip fryer basket. The last of the day's chips lay greasy and forlorn in the basket's bottom. These too, Abraham consumed, picking them from the basket with his bare hands.

His meal finished, Abraham turned his attention to other matters. It took him a while to figure out how to turn the lights off, but once done, he headed back upstairs and went to the bedroom. He lay down on the bed, ignoring the vague scent of body odor that wafted up from the dirty sheets. He felt exhausted. Drained. The food had helped, but he would need the watch to recover fully. Once he had it in his possession, he would find a suitable Victim and transfer their life force to himself. Actually, it would take several victims. A single killing would not suffice given the length of his entombment. Not if he wanted to regain his youth and strength. But all that could wait. Right now, he was simply happy to be out of the elements and out of sight. Abraham lay on the bed and stared at a patch of black mold on the ceiling, waiting for sleep to come, and wondering where Detective Inspector Abberline of Scotland Yard would have hidden what was rightfully his.

# SEVENTEEN

MINA HAD OVERSLEPT and now she was ten minutes late for her *Sociology of Crime* lecture. She ran up the steps of the William McDaniel building and pushed her way past a clutch of students lingering outside the main entrance. Once inside, she raced across the lobby, up a set of stairs to the second floor, and along a corridor until she reached the lecture hall. She entered as quietly as possible via the rear door and headed for a vacant seat.

"Pleased you could join us, Miss Parkinson." Her entrance had not escaped Prof. Edgerton, who fixed her with a steely glare from the podium.

"Sorry." Mina said, slightly out of breath. She sat down quickly and pulled an iPad out of her bag. "Overslept. It won't happen again."

"I should hope not," the professor said, unwilling to let her off the hook just yet. "You might consider investing in a good old-fashioned alarm clock. It will work much better than relying on your phone, I can assure you."

"I'll consider that, thank you." Mina hunkered down in her chair, uncomfortable with the gaze of a dozen or more students who'd turned to observe the object of the professor's wrath. She breathed a sigh of relief when Edgerton turned back to his chalkboard where he had posited the question; *does social standing and class predict the likelihood of a person resorting to crime?* Now he scrawled out a bullet list of talking points, explaining each as he went.

Mina's attention drifted. How could she focus on the sociology lecture when Jack the Ripper, recently resurrected from decades of slumber, was out there somewhere? The answer was simple. She couldn't. What she wanted to do was go in search of Callie Balfour and get access to the Ripper's den. Not that she had any idea how to accomplish that. She'd told Decker that Callie was a friend, but in reality, they'd only spoken a few times, and even then, only briefly. Callie was a postdoctoral researcher, much higher up on the ladder than Mina, and their interactions had mostly taken place within the classroom when Callie was giving a lecture. That didn't stop Mina from rushing out of the room the minute the lecture had concluded and going in search of her, finding the researcher right where she'd expected, in the bowels of the building. Mina took an elevator to the lower sub level and made her way along a dimly lit corridor with a records room and storage area flanking one side and a physics laboratory on the other until she arrived at the criminology department's basement research office. The door stood ajar, a thin sliver of light shining from within. She gave the door three light knocks.

"Yes?" A female voice drifted from beyond the door.

"I'm looking for Dr. Balfour?" Mina said through the crack.

"You're in luck then."

Mina lingered outside, waiting for some further confirmation that she had found Callie Balfour. When none came, she spoke through the door again. "Dr. Balfour?"

"I believe I've already confirmed that." Callie's voice drifted back to Mina. "Are you going to stand in the corridor all day, or would you prefer we talk face to face?"

"Oh. Right." Mina felt foolish. She pushed the door open and stepped inside.

The room looked like a hoarder with a crime fetish had taken up residence. There were books piled haphazardly on shelves, and even some stacked up on the floor. Storage boxes filled every available corner. There was even an antique shotgun leaning against a curio cabinet, as if its owner had just returned from the hunt.

Mina glanced at the gun. "That thing's not loaded, is it?"

"Don't be daft." Callie Balfour observed Mina with a bemused look upon her face. "It's been a hundred years since anyone fired it. The thing would probably blow up in your face if you tried."

"Good to know." Mina lingered in the doorway, awkward.

"I've seen you around campus before," Callie said. "You're American. A transfer student."

"Exchange student, actually."

"Well, whatever you are, I wish you'd come in and sit down." Callie motioned toward a chair on the opposite side of her desk. "You're making me rather nervous."

"Oh." Mina hurried to the chair and sat down, a little too hard. She was not handling this well so far and wondered why she was so flustered. Perhaps because she was keen to impress Decker. And also, because she didn't want to let him down after he had allowed her into his investigation.

Callie was studying her. "I assume there's a reason you came to see me?"

"Yes." Mina nodded. "It was your team that examined Jack the Ripper's room under that house in Mayfair."

"That's right." Callie looked suspicious. "Let me guess, you're going to ask if I'll show it to you."

"Well…"

"I thought so. You're the third one today. I practically had to call security to get rid of a spotty faced kid in the humanities building who claimed he was a descendant of Jack the Ripper. It's not possible, obviously, since no one knows the man's identity, but you have to give him marks for trying. I'll tell you what I told them. It's not possible."

"Just hear me out before you say no." Mina felt a surge of panic. "I have a valid reason, I promise."

"This should be interesting." Callie settled back in her chair. "I warn you, Jack's descendant set the bar pretty high."

"I know you think I'm just a student, but I'm actually working with an organization that might be able to identify Jack the Ripper. They've sent a couple of investigators to London for that very reason." Mina knew that she was fudging the truth. "It really is quite important that we get into that room."

"I see." Callie didn't look convinced. "If they're with a valid organization, why don't they make their requests through official channels?"

"It's…" Mina could feel herself being backed into a corner. She struggled to find an answer. "It's not that simple."

"It never is."

Mina sensed Callie was on the verge of asking her to leave. "They need to remain inconspicuous. They don't wish to draw attention to themselves."

"Ooh. How very cloak and dagger."

"They can help find your missing corpse." This was a Hail Mary, and Mina knew it. "The police haven't been much use, I bet."

"It doesn't seem to be their priority." Callie looked thoughtful. "You know what, I'll bite. If nothing else, it will break up the monotony of my day. How does 2 PM sound?"

"I'll ask them." Mina felt a surge of elation.

"Let me rephrase that. I'm free at 2 PM. Take it or leave it."

"We'll take it," Mina said. She eased her phone out of her pocket and glanced toward the screen. It was 10.45, and she had a lecture at eleven. "Thank you so much. You don't know what this means to me."

"I can guess by the look on your face." Callie smiled. "Word of advice. Never take up poker. You'll lose a lot of money."

"I'll remember that," Mina said.

"Good." Callie motioned toward the door. "Now scoot. I've got work to do, and I'm pretty sure you have a class."

# EIGHTEEN

IT WAS a little after ten in the morning when Decker woke up. He had barely cleared the sleep from his eyes when he heard a light knocking on the hotel room door. He dressed quickly and unlocked the door to find Colum waiting on the other side, the sling that he'd worn since their tangle with Grendel now conspicuous by its absence.

"Come on in," Decker said, then headed for the bathroom to freshen up. He left the door open and shouted back through it. "What happened to the sling?"

"Took it off. Damned thing was itchy and annoying."

"Are you sure that's wise?" Decker splashed water on his face, then exited the bathroom, drying himself with a towel as he did so. He flung the towel on the bed. "It hasn't been that long."

"It's fine. I've dealt with worse, believe me." Colum was standing near the window, gazing out toward the green expanse of Hyde Park. "The sling isn't coming back."

"Suit yourself." Decker shrugged. "Did you have any luck with those property records?"

"I think I've found him," Colum said, turning toward Decker. "It took some digging. I had to sign up to a couple of genealogy websites in order to access the census records for 1880s London, but we have a suspect."

"Really?" Decker raised an eyebrow. He headed for the coffeemaker and set about fixing his morning beverage. "That was quick."

"I was up til 4 AM, but it was worth it. Fascinating stuff."

"You want a coffee?" Decker asked, wondering how Colum looked so awake.

"Not on your life," Colum replied. "I can't stand hotel room coffee. Pure swill. I'll wait."

"Fair enough. You want to fill me in on what you found out?" Decker asked. "Did you get a name?"

"Abraham Turner." Colum replied. "At least that's the name recorded as the building's owner on the property records for that period. He's also listed on the 1881 census, where he lists himself as the only member of the household and his age as thirty-six."

"That puts him in a reasonable age range to be the Whitechapel killer."

"That it does. Here's where it gets more interesting. I couldn't find any relevant records in the 1871 census, but there's an Abraham Turner living at that address in each of the three decades prior to that, going all the way back to the 1841 census where he also lists his age as thirty-six."

"It's intriguing, I'll admit, but it doesn't prove that we found the identity of a vampiric Jack the Ripper. For all we know, his father shared the same name."

"True. But by the time the 1891 census rolls around, Abraham Turner has disappeared. There is no mention of him in subsequent records."

"Which would make sense if he was trapped in a cellar," Decker said. The coffee was ready. He picked it up and took a swig, then grimaced. "Holy cow, that's bad."

"Don't say I didn't warn you," Colum said with a grin. "There's a Costa Coffee in the lobby. My treat."

"That's very generous considering you'll probably expense it to Adam Hunt," Decker said with a laugh as they left the room and made their way to the elevator.

"I'm Irish, hospitality is in my nature," Colum replied. "Even if someone else is picking up the tab."

"In that case, I'm getting a Danish too." Decker let Colum step into the elevator first, then followed. They rode down to the lobby and made their way to the coffee shop. While they waited for their beverages, Decker returned to the subject of the house on Hay's Mews. "I'm curious. What happened to the property after Abraham Turner vanished?"

"Nothing." Colum shrugged. "I couldn't find any further information on the building or its occupants for decades after the 1881 census. There are no records of sale, no birth or death certificates listing anyone at that address, no marriage certificates. It's like the property just stood there, unoccupied and forgotten."

"Adam Hunt mentioned an organization that hunted the Ripper and surreptitiously took care of the issue. A precursor to CUSP. Maybe they took control of the property."

"That's as good a theory as any," Colum admitted. "It would make sense. They would want to ensure the house didn't fall into the wrong hands to keep Jack's subterranean prison from being discovered. Looks like they were successful too. At least until 1941, when the street took a direct hit from a German incendiary bomb, all but destroying several of the buildings, including Jack's house. That's where the records pick up again. They rebuilt the structures on Hay's Mews after the war."

"And when a separate incendiary bomb destroyed all our predecessor's records, the secret of the Ripper's true identity and his location were lost to time."

"Until those workers broke down that wall a few days ago and discovered the hidden room."

"Precisely," Colum said.

Their coffees had arrived. Decker was about to take one, when his phone rang. He answered. It was Mina. After he hung up, he turned to Colum. "Good news. Mina got us into the Ripper's lair."

"Do you think we'll find anything useful there?" Colum asked.

"I have no idea," Decker admitted. "But if nothing else, it's a place to start."

# NINETEEN

DETECTIVE INSPECTOR ELLIOT MEAD looked down at the mutilated girl sprawled before him. She lay with one leg twisted under the other, her arms stretched out as if she were greeting death with a hug. Her dead eyes stared into the ashen sky, glazed and sightless. Blood had pooled around her in a macabre halo.

"How long has she been here?" He asked, addressing a plump woman who kneeled next to the body. The forensic pathologist, replete in white overalls and purple gloves, might have been indistinguishable from the scene of crime officers who were combing the surrounding area, except the focus of her attention was inward to the victim rather than outward to the wider landscape.

"Less than twenty-four hours." The pathologist glanced up toward Elliot. "If you had to pin me down, I would put the time of death as sometime around midnight yesterday, or perhaps the early hours of this morning. That's considering rigor mortis, lividity, and the temperature overnight."

Elliott nodded. He glanced beyond the flapping crime scene tape that blocked off entry to the patch of wasteland. There were two points of access, one from a narrow alleyway that ran between two tall buildings, and also an access road that led onto a residential street containing blocks of flats, and further down, the start of the university campus. Beyond the barrier, and the police officers that guarded it, he could see a throng of curious people. Gawkers attracted by the spectacle. Others, the closest, were journalists. Many of them represented newspapers both local and further afield, but three or four stood in front of TV cameras, talking breathlessly and gesturing. Bad news traveled fast. The murder would be all over the six o'clock news.

He turned his attention from the ghoulish onlookers and studied his surroundings. The buildings on the alleyway side were offices, so there would be no point in canvassing there for witnesses given the likely time of the attack. No one would be working that late. The blocks of flats might be a different story, but they were far away, and none directly overlooked the crime scene. Of the buildings that backed up onto the vacant plot of land, only a few had rear windows that faced him, and he wasn't holding his breath for a lucky break. The likelihood was that no one was looking out given the late hour, and even if they were, it would have been pitch black and almost impossible to see anything. And he already knew there were no CCTV cameras close by. This was the perfect place to commit murder. Especially since it provided an easy shortcut for students returning to the university housing nearby from a night on the town. This poor girl probably died because she wanted to shave ten minutes from her walk. Little did she know that there was a predator lying in wait amid the rubble of what had once been a 1960s era office block. If the developers got planning permission, there would be another building here before long, and that would mean ample lighting and security cameras. But for now, it was his worst nightmare, a metaphorical Venus fly trap luring the unwary. There had been a rape and two robberies on this patch of land already this year. Now he could add homicide to that list. Worse, it was not the first murder. Another girl had turned up dead only a few days before in a Mayfair alleyway, also with her throat cut. Was there a fledgling serial killer wandering the streets of London? Elliott hoped not. Maybe it was just a coincidence. But his instincts and years on the job told him otherwise. There would be more bodies before this was over, he was sure. The only question was, how many?

# TWENTY

DECKER AND COLUM arrived at the townhouse on Hays Mews a few minutes before two in the afternoon. When they got there, Mina was already waiting. Next to her stood a diminutive blonde woman that appeared to be in her mid-twenties, and a beanpole of a kid whose skin was so pasty white Decker wondered if he'd ever seen the sun for more than an hour at a time. As they approached the group, Mina waved, a grin plastered across her face.

"You're early." Mina said.

"So are you," Decker pointed out. He glanced across the road toward the alleyway they had investigated the previous evening. The crime scene tape was still there, but one side had detached, and it now lay trailing across the pavement.

"Duh. There's no way I'd be late for this." She let out a squeal of excitement. "This is where Jack the Ripper lived. I'd have camped on the sidewalk for a month to see this if I had to."

"Well, it's a good job that won't be necessary then," Decker said with a smile. "I hear it gets quite chilly in London in the fall."

"It can be a little nippy," the blond woman said, speaking for the first time. She stepped forward and extended a hand. "I'm Doctor Callie Balfour."

"Pleased to make your acquaintance." Decker took her hand and shook it. "You must be Mina's friend at the university."

"Mina and I have crossed paths a few times, mostly during lectures," Callie said without missing a beat. "I'm a postdoctoral researcher in the criminology department. My specialty is in historical crimes."

"Hence your interest in Jack the Ripper," Decker said.

"Naturally. It is one of the most intriguing unsolved crimes in history." Callie's eyes strayed toward Colum. She looked him up and down appreciatively. "You haven't introduced me to your friend yet."

"My name would be Colum, ma'am. It's a pleasure."

"You're Irish."

"Indeed, I am." Colum flashed a row of white teeth. "You won't hold that against me now, will you?"

"We'll see." Now it was Callie's turn to smile. She motioned toward the young man at her side. "This is my research assistant, Martin Slade."

"Hi." Martin said, then glanced shyly at Mina. "We share a couple of classes."

Mina nodded. "I know. You sit behind me in sociology."

Martin nodded and smiled. "That's right. I've been wanting to talk to you but hadn't gotten the courage up."

"Well, now you have." Mina blushed.

Callie ignored her assistant's fumbling attempts at flirtation. She looked at Decker and Colum. "Would you two chaps like to peek inside Jack the Ripper's lair?"

"We can't wait," Mina said, giving no one else a chance to reply.

"Follow me then." Callie unlocked the door and pushed it open. She stepped inside and waited for the others before heading down the hallway toward the door at the back of the house.

The interior smelled like sawed wood. The walls were torn back to the studs, the staircase partially dismantled. Discarded tools lay here and there, and in what remained of the living room, stood a table saw. Decker wondered why the work wasn't continuing, and how Callie came to have a set of keys.

As if reading his mind, Callie stopped at the cellar door and turned toward them. "The owner of this house has graciously allowed us to conduct research on the premises prior to completing his renovation. We have access to the cellar for another week before work resumes."

"What will happen after that?" Mina asked.

"I don't know." Callie opened the cellar door and started downward. When they reached the bottom, she led them to the back wall where a dark hole yawned. A pile of bricks marked the secret room's discovery. "I'd like to think they will preserve this chamber for posterity. There has been some talk of keeping it intact in case they want to offer tours of the house at some point. This building has gained an aura of notoriety almost overnight. There's a lot of interest."

"I can see why," Decker said. "Jack the Ripper has captivated people for generations."

"Captivated?" Callie said as she turned on a pair of portable work lights. "More like obsessed. Isn't that right, Martin?"

"A little obsession isn't a bad thing," Martin replied. "Besides, this truly is fascinating. Think about where we are. The Whitechapel killer could have stood right here, on the very stones under my feet."

"Martin practically begged me to put him on the team," Callie said. "He did his undergraduate dissertation on the Ripper."

"Sounds like we have a Ripperologist in our midst," Colum said.

"Make that two," Mina replied. "I always wanted to visit London just to see Whitechapel."

"Are we going to stand here chatting all day, or would you like to see what we came here for?" Callie motioned toward the hole in the wall, and the room beyond which was now lit by the work lamps.

"Of course." Decker stepped over the pile of bricks and into the room. It was larger than he imagined, with walls of old brick and a ceiling supported by stout wooden beams. Dust and cobwebs filled every corner. The air smelled old and musty. In the center of the room was a table, and beyond it a chair made of wood.

"That's where we found the body." Callie nodded toward the chair. "He was sitting there just staring at the door as if he wished he could escape."

"That's exactly what happened," Mina said.

"Don't remind me," Callie said ruefully. "The police are still no closer to finding him than they were the night he disappeared. Thank goodness we removed the handcuffs first."

"Handcuffs?" Colum raised an eyebrow.

"Yes. The corpse was sitting with his hands behind his back, wrists shackled together with a pair of golden handcuffs."

"When you say golden…"

"I mean exactly that. The cuffs are solid gold. We have them back at the university."

"They must be worth a small fortune," Colum said. "I hope you're keeping them secure."

"They're in a fireproof safe back at my office," Callie said. "I'm not taking chances with anything of such historical and monetary value."

"Good to hear." Decker was looking around the room, taking in every detail. "What else did you find here?"

"A knife," Callie replied. She pointed toward the table. "It was sitting right there, as if he'd used it only yesterday. It was creepy, to be honest."

"It still had blood on it," Martin said, his eyes sparkling with excitement. "Can you believe that? After all those years, the blood of his victims was still dried onto the blade."

"That's horrible," Mina said with a shiver. "I can't imagine what it must have been like to die in such a manner."

"I know. Right?" Martin walked over to the table and reached out, touching its wooden surface with an almost reverent respect. "To feel that blade sliding across your bare skin. Slicing down to the bone as the blood drains from your body. Just think about it."

"I'd rather not, mate, if that's all the same with you," Colum said. He glanced at Decker. "I'm not sure there's much that can help us here."

"I agree," Decker said. He turned to Callie. "Thank you for letting us see the room. We appreciate it."

"My pleasure," Callie said. "Mina mentioned that you work for an investigative organization. Would you mind telling me who?"

"I'm afraid we can't do that," Decker replied.

"I figured as much. You look like spooks, although for the life of me I can't imagine why government agents would have any interest in this." Callie shook her head and smiled ruefully. "I suppose I should have asked before I let you down here."

"Probably," Decker admitted.

"You still wouldn't have told me though, would you?"

"Nope, but I might have come up with a plausible story to bluff my way in."

"Well, at least you're honest." Callie folded her arms. "Was Mina telling the truth when she said you could help me find Jack's body?"

"We have every intention of finding Jack's body," Colum said. "I assure you of that."

"Well that's something, then." Callie nodded toward the door. "If you gentlemen are quite done, I have a busy afternoon."

"I think we've seen everything we need to." Decker dug into his pocket and removed a pair of business cards, blank except for his name and a phone number that would route through to the phone Adam Hunt had given him in Ireland. This was not the phone's real number, but rather a virtual one that was impossible to trace and changeable at will. On the back of the card he wrote the name of their hotel and his room. He handed one card to Callie, and the second to her assistant, Martin. "If anything comes up, please contact me."

"I can't imagine I'll need to," Callie said, pushing the card into her purse. "But I'll hang on to it, just in case. I assume you'll call me if you find my missing corpse?"

"Naturally." Decker watched Martin tuck the other card into his inside coat pocket. "You have my word."

# TWENTY-ONE

ABRAHAM TURNER STOOD at the chip shop's second-floor window and peered down on the street below. He hated being confined to the cramped apartment and had paced back and forth for most of the morning and into the afternoon. He was restless. Bored. Most of all, he was disgusted by his own appearance, which had been revealed earlier that day when he stepped into the cramped and filthy bathroom. The man staring back at him in the mirror was hardly recognizable. A dried up and grotesque husk with skin pulled like aging parchment over a framework of bones and shriveled muscle. At least he wasn't still wearing the same tattered garb that had graced his back for more than a century. He had discarded his soiled and ripped clothing for more suitable attire as soon as he discovered the wardrobe full of clothes in the bedroom. It was pure luck that the man he'd killed had a similar enough build, although the trousers were a couple of sizes too large, held up by a tightly cinched belt, and the shirt he now wore felt baggy. Once he got hold of the fob watch and the amulet hidden within, things would be different. He would once more be able to revivify his wasted muscles, bring life back to his withered flesh, and extend his already centuries long life once more. That someone else would have to die to achieve this did not bother him any more than the thousands he'd already slain.

Abraham turned away from the window and stepped back into the room, tired of watching the hustle and bustle of the crowded city. Despite his sour mood, one thing lifted Abraham's spirits. His voice was returning. After being locked in silence for so long, it was not surprising that his vocal cords had failed to respond when called upon. Now though, the feeble rattling sounds that escaped his throat whenever he attempted to speak had given way to words, albeit raspy and quiet. It was not the booming voice he'd once possessed, but that, like everything else, would come back to him in time.

Abraham sat on the couch. On the floor below, the chip shop was locked up and quiet. Earlier that morning, he'd written a sign for the front window. *Closed until further notice.* This would deter hungry patrons and keep his new hideout secure, at least for a while. He'd slept in a bed for the first time in a hundred and thirty years and had no desire to end up back at the partially collapsed building that had once been the Marsden Street Workhouse.

He studied the coffee table and the pile of curious objects resting upon it. There was a magazine, the paper shiny and crisp with images so real he thought they might jump off the page. He picked it up, thumbed through it and then discarded it again. The entire publication was devoted to the horseless carriages called automobiles. He picked up a carton with Chinese lettering on the side and a wire handle at the top. The inside was greasy and caked with scraps of rice. A fork lay nearby, similarly encrusted with the remains of the chip shop owners last meal. He put the cartoon back on the table, his interest piqued by another item. A small oblong box. Buttons adorned its face with symbols Abraham didn't recognize. He picked it up, turned it over in his hands, then pressed a button. Nothing. He pressed a couple more, but still its purpose evaded him. Near the top was a larger red button. When he pressed this, something happened, but at first, he wasn't sure what.

The room filled with noise. Voices. Abraham dropped the box and jumped to his feet, alarmed. Had the authorities discovered him? Were there agents of whatever organization had condemned him to a century long sleep storming up the stairs even now? But no. When he went to the door and peered down the toward the first floor, he discovered that he was still alone. Abraham turned back into the room, relieved. It was then that he discovered the source of the noise. A box attached to the wall - until now a blank and featureless piece of glass - had come alive with moving pictures.

Abraham returned to the sofa and sat back down, never taking his eyes off the wondrous sight. He picked up the oblong box again and played with the buttons, noting how the sound got louder and softer, or the picture changed, depending on which buttons he pressed. He sat transfixed, moving between channels, and pausing on those that intrigued him. He witnessed wars and arguments. A soccer game. A band playing, the music discordant and ugly. At one point he came across a woman selling jewelry, the prices absurdly inflated and her wares ridiculously tacky.

Then he arrived at one particular channel that gave him pause. A banner scrolled across the bottom of the screen. *Second body discovered with throat cut. Serial killer on the loose.* A cute brunette with sparkling blue eyes looked out at him, although he didn't think she knew he was staring back at her. And all the while she talked about the vicious killings that had occurred. Two young women brutally murdered within the last three days. Panic gripped the city. Abraham settled back on the sofa and watched with spellbound glee.

# TWENTY-TWO

CALLIE BALFOUR HAD SPENT the rest of the afternoon in a lecture after leaving John Decker and his companions at the house on Hay's Mews. It was now six in the evening as she returned to her basement office to finish grading a batch of tests before heading home. She also wanted to take another look at the Ripper's knife. A thought had occurred to her while they were down in the Whitechapel murderer's den. If the knife carried century-old blood, it was possible the killer himself had left DNA evidence behind. If so, they might link it to known genetic material recovered from the crime scenes, such as the shawl found near the body of the Ripper's fourth victim, Catherine Eddowes. Since the shawl contained trace evidence from both the victim and the killer, it would prove beyond any doubt that the Whitechapel murderer had lived in the house on Hay's Mews. Even better, they could confirm that the corpse in the cellar was Jack, thus solving the mystery of why the murder spree had stopped so suddenly. Except they didn't have the body, a fact that made Callie clench her fists in frustration every time she thought about it. They had been so close. Callie was still pondering this when she arrived at the office.

Martin was there, although he was about to leave. He was zipping his coat when she entered.

"I wasn't expecting you back today," he said. "I'm just about to head out."

"It's fine, I don't need you." Callie went to her desk and sat down. "I have some papers to grade and then I'll be out of here myself."

"I don't mind staying." Martin lingered near the door. "I don't have any plans this evening."

"No. You go." Callie looked around her desk, expecting to see the knife there. She saw no sign of it. She glanced up at Martin. "But before you do, have you seen the Ripper's knife? I was sure I left on my desk, but it doesn't seem to be here now."

Martin paused for a moment, then nodded. "I put in the back room with the other artifacts. Didn't want to leave it lying around."

"Thanks." Callie pushed her chair back to stand up.

"Don't trouble yourself. I'll get it." Martin waved her back down. "Is there anything else you want while I'm back there?"

"Just the knife." Callie watched Martin disappear into the back storage room. She heard him rummaging around, and then he returned a moment later, holding a plastic evidence bag with the knife inside.

"Safe and sound." Martin placed the knife on her desk. "Don't stay too late. I know what you're like when you get lost in the past."

"I have no intention of staying late. Half an hour and I'm out of here." Callie pulled the knife toward her and looked at it through the clear plastic bag. "I have a date with a soaking tub and a glass of chardonnay this evening, I think."

"Sounds lovely. Make sure you keep that date." Martin moved toward the door. He reached for the handle, but before he could leave there came a light knock. He glanced at Callie. "Looks like we have a visitor."

"Then open the door and see who it is." Callie hoped the girl, Mina, hadn't come back to ask for another favor.

She hadn't. It was a woman around Callie's age with jet black hair tied into a bun behind her head.

"Are you Callie Balfour?" The woman's voice was soft with the faintest hint of a West Country accent.

"Yes, that's me." Callie was on her guard. Since finding Jack's den, her office had been a revolving door for journalists, the curious, and the morbidly obsessed. "Can I help you?"

"I hope so." The woman stepped into the room, casting a quick glance toward Martin as she did so. "My name is Stephanie Gleason. I saw you in the local paper."

"The article about Jack the Ripper's home in Mayfair, I assume," Callie said.

"Yes, indeed." Stephanie approached the desk.

"If you're here to gain access to the Ripper's lair, I'm afraid you're wasting your time," Callie said. "The site is off limits to the public."

"Oh, goodness. It's nothing like that, I assure you."

"How can I help you then, Miss Gleason?" Callie sat back in her chair and observed the newcomer, hoping she wasn't dealing with a Ripper fanatic or some other deranged person.

"It's more what I can do for you." Stephanie looked around the room until her eyes eventually settled upon the knife lying on Callie's desk. "I'm the great-great-granddaughter of Thomas Finch."

"Who?" Callie asked, confused.

"Colonel Thomas Finch. He was an unofficial associate of Detective Inspector Abberline of Scotland Yard during the Whitechapel murders. I suppose you might describe him as an advisor, but he was so much more."

"I've never heard of him." Callie shook her head.

"What about the Order of St. George?"

Again, Callie shook her head. "I've never heard of them either."

"Are you quite sure?" A look of distress passed across Stephanie's face. "Lives may depend on it."

"One hundred percent." Callie's heart sank. This woman was clearly just another wacko. She contemplated calling campus security. "Would you mind telling me what this has to do with the Ripper?"

"I'm sorry." Stephanie was backing toward the door now. "I must have made a mistake. I assumed you were part of the Order, given your position at the university and interest in the Ripper. I was wrong."

"If you'll tell me about this group, perhaps I can help you." Callie's was curious, even though she suspected that her visitor was delusional.

"I'm not at liberty to discuss that. Maybe they don't even exist anymore. If they did, I'm sure they would've contacted you by now." Stephanie was at the door. She turned and looked back. "I'm sorry to have bothered you."

Callie watched her leave, then turned back to her work.

Martin had said nothing throughout the entire exchange, but now he spoke up. "Well, *she* was wackadoodle. Chalk another one up to the mystique of the Ripper."

"She was a little odd." Callie said. Then she remembered John Decker and Colum O'Shea. Mina had described them as a couple of investigators who wished to remain inconspicuous. Were they somehow linked to this group Stephanie Gleason was looking for? Callie pushed her chair back and stood up.

"Where are you going?" Martin asked.

"I need a breath of fresh air," Callie replied. She didn't want to say what she was thinking out loud. It was just a hunch, and if it didn't pan out, no one would be any the wiser. "It's stuffy down here."

Martin shrugged. "FYI, I'll be gone when you get back. I've had enough of this place for one day."

"Sure." Callie nodded. "Have a good evening."

She left the office and hurried along the corridor. She took the staircase to the first floor two steps at a time and ran through the building's lobby and out onto the quadrangle. There were a few students strolling along the gravel pathways that cut through the quad's meticulously kept grass. It didn't take her long to spot Stephanie Gleason walking toward the road.

She took off at a sprint and closed the gap between them, calling out to attract the other woman's attention once she was within earshot.

Stephanie turned, stopping when she saw Callie running toward her. "Did you remember something?" She asked.

"Yes." Callie came to a halt, breathless. "I think I can help you, after all."

# TWENTY-THREE

AT EIGHT O'CLOCK THAT EVENING, Decker and Colum caught a taxi to the university campus to meet Callie Balfour. The call had come in an hour before on Decker's phone. A breathless Callie had asked if they could come over to the university right away. There was a woman that they would want to meet. She had information pertinent to his investigation into Jack the Ripper, although when he pressed her to elaborate, Callie became tightlipped. Apparently, the mystery woman would only speak to them in person and had not confided in Callie other than to assure her it was a matter of utmost importance.

When they arrived, Mina was waiting for them on the quadrangle in front of the William McDaniel building. She met them with a hug, practically hopping from foot to foot with unrestrained glee.

"This is so cool," Mina said. "A real-life clandestine liaison."

"It's just a regular meeting," Decker said to curb Mina's enthusiasm. "Nothing to get excited about."

"Easy for you to say," Mina shot back. "I've been doing nothing but study for a year. This is the most exciting thing that's happened to me since Shackleton."

"There's nothing wrong with studying." Decker led them across the quadrangle toward the building. He mounted the steps and held the door open for Mina and Colum, then followed them in. He glanced toward Mina. "Callie said to meet in her office. I assume you know where that is?"

"What do you think?" Mina led them across the lobby to the elevator. They stepped inside and she pressed a button marked sub-basement.

"They keep her in the basement?" Colum asked. "I guess she doesn't have the highest standing around here."

"I think it's cool." When the elevator door opened Mina stepped out into a dimly lit corridor with doors on both sides. "Follow me."

They made their way toward the furthest door, passing a laboratory and several storage rooms on the way. When they reached their destination, Mina came to a halt and knocked twice.

"Come in." A voice answered.

Decker pushed the door open and stepped inside with the others crowding behind. Callie was sitting behind a cluttered desk stacked high with paperwork. A woman Decker hadn't seen before occupied a chair on the other side.

The stranger glanced up. "You must be John Decker."

"And you are?"

Callie motioned to the woman sitting opposite her. "This is Stephanie Gleason."

"Pleased to meet you, Miss Gleason. How may we be of service?"

"It's more how I can be of service to you, Mr. Decker. Assuming you are whom I suspect you to be."

"And who would that be," Colum asked.

"Ah yes. The Irishman. Callie told me about you."

"The name's Colum O'Shea. You still haven't answered my question."

"Then I'll get right to the point. Do you know of a man named Thomas Finch?"

Colum and Decker exchanged glances. Adam Hunt had mentioned this very name during their briefing on the way to the airport.

"What about him?" Decker asked.

"I'll take that as a yes." Stephanie nodded but showed no other outward sign of emotion. "Thomas Finch was instrumental in stopping the serial killer known as Jack the Ripper back in 1889."

"We know that much," Colum said. He glanced toward Callie. "Before we say anything else, I need to know if we can trust everyone in the room."

"If by that generalized and sweeping statement, you mean me, then yes you can." Callie said with a scowl. "Might I remind you that this meeting wouldn't even be happening if I hadn't arranged it."

"I don't like this," Colum said to Decker. "There are too many civilians getting involved."

"You don't even know what I have to say yet." Stephanie stood up. "If you're not interested, I can leave."

"No, don't do that." Mina took a step toward the table. "I'm sorry about my friends, they can be a bit gruff."

"I might be many things," Colum said. "But one thing I'm not, is gruff."

"Yeah, you kind of are." Mina grinned at the big Irishman. "But don't worry, it's cute. I like it."

"That's enough," Decker said. He could sense the meeting spinning out of control and they hadn't even found out why they were here yet. "Mina, put a sock in it."

Colum smirked but said nothing.

"If we've all finished butting heads, could we get back to business," Callie said. "I'd rather not be here all night."

"We should call Adam and get his authorization before we proceed any further," Colum said, reaching for his phone.

"There's no need," Decker said. "He sent us here to do a job, and I'm going to do it the way I see fit. Besides, we have no idea how long it would take to get authorization once we put this through official channels."

"You seem to be forgetting I'm the senior agent," Colum said. For good measure he added, "and I outrank you in the organization."

"Really." Decker raised an eyebrow. "Hunt mentioned nothing about you outranking me. In fact, he hasn't brought up rank at all. I thought we were partners. Still, no matter. I shall bow to your superior knowledge. What would you like to do?"

Colum pushed the phone back into his pocket. "I think we should proceed without involving Adam Hunt. As you pointed out, he sent us here to take care of the situation. And it would be a shame to lose a vital intel just because we were waiting for authorization from thousands of miles away."

"See, now you're talking like a real field agent." Decker slapped Colum on the back. "I'll break you out of that company man routine yet."

"I've seen married couples that bicker less than the pair of you," Callie said, staring at the two men in disbelief. "Are you done?"

Colum looked sheepish. "Before we proceed, I must get assurances that nothing we say will pass beyond those present in this room."

"Fine. Whatever." Callie rolled her eyes. "I agree."

"So do I." Stephanie observed the two men with a stony gaze. "And now that's all behind us, there's something I need to know."

"What would that be?" Colum asked.

"Are you, or are you not, members of the Order of St. George?"

Silence fell upon the room.

The question hung in the air, and then Colum cleared his throat and spoke. "We are not."

"Dammit." Stephanie reached down to pick up a backpack that had been leaning against her chair. She stepped toward the door. "I'm sorry to have wasted your time. If you're not with the Order, then I'm afraid our meeting is over."

"Whoa." Decker blocked her path. "I think there's been a misunderstanding. When Colum said that we are not in the Order of St. George, he was technically correct. We aren't. Because they haven't existed since the Second World War. We represent the organization that they became after that time. We're as close to the Order as you will ever get."

Stephanie hesitated and turned back. "If what you say is true, then you'll know why Jack the Ripper was walled up in that room."

"Because they couldn't kill him," Colum said. He turned to Callie.

"No one stole your corpse. It got up and walked out of that room all on its own. Jack the Ripper isn't dead."

"What?" Callie shook her head in disbelief. "Don't be absurd."

"He's not being absurd." Stephanie walked back to the desk. She put the backpack down atop it. "The Ripper is out there right now. He's already killed, and he will do it again. That's why I sought you out."

"This is all very well," Decker said. "But you still haven't said why you needed to speak with us so urgently."

"To show you this." Stephanie unzipped the backpack and reached inside. She lifted out a square container a little smaller than a shoebox. It glinted golden under the room's weak light as she placed it on the table. She opened the lid and reached inside, removing a fob watch that hung on a silver chain. "He'll stop at nothing to get it, so we have to make sure he never does."

# TWENTY-FOUR

THE APARTMENT above the chip shop was dark and quiet. Abraham Turner was in the bedroom, laying on the narrow bed amid the sweat stained sheets with his eyes closed. He wasn't fully asleep, but dozing fitfully. From somewhere outside there was the high-pitched bleat of a car's horn, followed by the revving of an engine. But Abraham paid it no heed, he was in another time and place.

Marston Moor.

The year was 1644 and there was a brutal civil war raging. Abraham, who was already several hundred years old at that point, had found a home among the Parliamentarians, also known as the Roundheads, under the command of Oliver Cromwell. For the last three months they had laid siege to the city of York, desperate to curtail royalist power in the north of England. Now things had come to a head. They had finally engaged the Royalists that very evening in a surprise attack. Two hours later the ground was thick with corpses and the Royalists, what remained of them, were in retreat. Not that Abraham cared which side won or lost. He was above the petty squabbles that decided who would rule the land for a few years until the next disagreement broke out. All he cared about was the blood, and there was plenty of it.

He wandered the battlefield now the fight was over. He picked his way through the dead and dying, ignoring the sobs of the mortally wounded and their pitiful cries for help. Occasionally he would stoop next to an injured man and pull his head from the mud, examine his wounds, but most were too far gone to be of use. He was looking for those whose life force had not yet faded, those who might survive their injuries, although he had no intention of letting them live. When he found such an unfortunate, he kneeled beside him, took out his knife, and pressed the blade against the man's neck, ignoring his terrified pleas for mercy. That his victim was a parliamentarian, a man who'd fought beside Abraham only hours earlier, was of no consequence. He was loyal only to whichever force afforded a better opportunity. It was the Roundheads today, but in the past, he'd marched alongside the Celts, the Anglo-Saxons, and even the Roman Ninth Legion.

The death of the man lying in the mud beneath him would, in some measure, ensure Abraham lived to fight many more battles for centuries to come. He looked into the frightened man's eyes, his knife not yet breaking the skin. He could feel his victim's life force, still strong. Soon it would flow from this doomed man into Abraham.

"Please sir, I beg you, help me," The man gasped. A trickle of blood meandered down his face from a previously inflicted head wound, perhaps delivered by a mace or the hilt of the sword.

"I'll put an end to your pain, if that will help," Abraham said.

"Why?" The man asked, clearly confused that one of his own would wish to do him such harm.

Abraham ignored the question. There was little use in explaining his motivation to what was, essentially, a talking corpse. Instead, he pressed the knife down and drew it back in a swift and smooth motion.

The man's eyes bulged, and his lips drew back in a pained grimace, as the blade bit into his neck, opening his windpipe and severing his jugular. Blood, which until now had escaped the wounded man at a leisurely pace, now departed his body in a torrent.

Abraham's pulse quickened. He reached under his shirt and removed the amulet he wore around his neck, a circular flat disk of carved stone chiseled with a design older than even he could remember. It hung on a leather cord, low enough that when concealed beneath his clothing it sat against his chest. Now he held it out and bent low, his tongue pushing into the ragged wound caused by his knife. The soldier beneath him moaned, a low cry of desperation born out of the knowledge that he would soon be dead. He raised his hand and tried to pull Abraham away, but he was too weak. Instead, the hand just rested on Abraham's back as he lapped the man's torn neck.

Abraham pulled away and watched for a moment as his victim's head lolled to one side. He would expire soon. Abraham lifted the talisman to his mouth, ran his tongue across the rough stone, and deposited the dying man's blood upon it.

All at once he felt a jolt. A surge of energy that leaped from the talisman and into his very core. He threw his head back, exulting in the rush as another man's life poured into him, keeping him young and transferring all the years his victim would never know. He gritted his teeth against the sudden pain as every nerve in his body lit with invisible fire and his muscles spasmed. But it was a brief discomfort, the price he must pay for stealing another man's life.

Abraham slipped the pendant back under his shirt and glanced down. The man whose throat he'd cut stared up with wide dead eyes. From somewhere off to his left, he heard movement. Abraham stood up and turned to see another man picking his way through the field of corpses. The newcomer turned to look at him and their eyes met. In shared understanding. Abraham was not the only vulture on the battlefield that day. He raised a hand in greeting. But then the dream was fading, spinning away into silvery strands that dissipated into a black void. A chasm that soon collapsed upon itself and became the walls of a cramped room above a chip shop in London.

---

Abraham sat up with a gasp, the last remnants of his dream fading into the ether. He felt a momentary pang of sadness for a past lost forever.

But then he felt something else.

An overwhelming sense of place. But not the room he now occupied. This place was further away. The trickling stream of awareness had become a raging torrent. His lost watch, which he'd only perceived as if through a thick and disorienting fog until now, was calling him.

Abraham swung his legs off the bed and stood up. He closed his eyes for a moment, focusing his mind. Then he strode from the room and down the stairs, exiting the chip shop through the back door. He knew where the watch was now, and it was time he got it back.

# TWENTY-FIVE

STEPHANIE GLEASON HELD the watch up. It glinted in the glow from the overhead lights, twisting back and forth on its chain. "This has been in my family since the time of my great-great-grandfather, passed down through the generations. It has been our sacred duty to guard it and to wait."

"Wait for what?" Mina asked.

"For Jack the Ripper to reappear. The Order didn't want the watch to fall into the wrong hands. Their reliquary could not protect it, so they entrusted my ancestor to its safekeeping."

"And your ancestor would be?" Colum asked.

"Thomas Finch," Decker said, answering for her.

"Yes. He was an original member of the Order, handpicked by Queen Victoria herself. He eventually became its leader, but that was many years after the Whitechapel murders."

"He must've been a fascinating man," Decker said.

"He was. At least if you believe my grandmother's stories."

"So, what's the deal with the gold box?" Mina asked.

"It's for protection. The walls are inch-thick lead wrapped in gold leaf. It's kind of like a supernatural cloaking device. The Ripper can't find it as long as the watch remains in the box."

"And yet you're holding it up for us to see," Colum said.

"I'm sure it will be fine for a few moments," Stephanie replied, but regardless, a nervous twitch pulsed at the corner of her eye. "It's important you see it so you will understand."

"Understand what?" Decker asked. "It appears to be an ordinary watch."

"Looks can be deceptive, Mr. Decker." Stephanie placed the timepiece on the table before she turned it over and opened the back. Inside, concealed within the watch's silver case, was a round stone disk that accounted for half the watch's depth.

"I've never seen anything like that before," Colum said, leaning forward to get a better view.

"Me either." Callie reached out. "Would you mind if I take a closer look?"

"Not at all," Stephanie said, sliding the watch across the desk. "But be quick. I don't want to leave it out of the box for long."

"This is fascinating." Callie picked up the watch and stared at the hidden disk within. "It looks like there's a design etched into the surface of the stone."

"Why would anyone hide a piece of stone in the back of a watch?" Colum rubbed his chin thoughtfully. "I can't imagine it has anything to do with the workings of the timepiece itself."

"It doesn't," Callie said. She inserted a fingernail between the rim of the watch and the disk and lifted, plucking it out with two fingers. "It's a tight fit, but it's just sitting in there."

"The purpose of the watch is to hide the disk, nothing more." Decker said. "The question is, why would anyone want to hide it?"

"So that they could keep it on their person without drawing attention?" Colum speculated.

"It wasn't always in the watch." Callie was holding the disk up. She ran her fingers around its rim until she came to a small hole that pierced the disk near the edge. "It must've been on a chain or necklace at some point."

"It's a piece of jewelry?" Mina asked.

"I don't think so. Not jewelry. The carvings on the disk look almost…" Callie struggled to find the right word. "Ceremonial. They remind me of carvings I've seen in books on ancient cultures like the Maya, or the Egyptians."

"You don't think-"

"No, it's neither of those. I would guess that this is from much closer to home and probably made in the British Isles. Although how old it is, I can't tell." Callie placed the disk back into the watch. "It reminds me of something, though. I'm sure I've seen this symbol somewhere before."

"Where?" Decker asked.

"Hang on a moment." Callie rummaged through the papers on her desk until she found a manila file folder. "I think I have it here. Come closer."

Everyone crowded around the desk as Callie opened the folder. Inside was a thin stack of photographs - all images of Jack's body sitting in the cellar. She flicked through them until she came to one particular image. A scrolling archaic design burned into the corpse's leathery skin, low on the inside of his wrist. She placed the photo next to the open watch. "I took this photo the day we discovered Jack's body in the cellar. Before it went missing. Look at the design. The two designs are the same in mirror image."

"I'll be damned." Colum shook his head. "I bet if you put that stone disk against the Ripper's wrist it will make an exact match."

"The question is, why?" Callie said.

"We'll answer that question when we find the Ripper." Colum said.

"I can help on that score too." Callie took a pair of photographs from the folder. She offered them to Decker. "This is what your killer looks like."

Decker took the photos. Abraham Turner had seen better days. His skin was brown and mummified. Tattered clothes clung to his wasted frame. Dead eyes looked out at the camera. He passed the photo to Colum and studied the second one. This time it was a closeup of the corpse's head, showing Abraham's grotesque countenance in vivid detail. Mottled and brown skin stretched tight over sunken features. Discolored and crooked teeth. The tip of a blackened tongue poked out through blackened lips that curled up in a rictus grin. Wiry clumps of dusty hair covered the dead man's scalp. Decker shuddered and passed the second photo to his partner.

"At least we know what he looks like now," Decker said.

"What an unpleasant chap," Colum commented. "He won't win any beauty contests."

"You can keep those. I have copies," Callie said. She closed the watch and passed it back to Stephanie. "I'm sorry, I'm still having trouble getting my head around the idea that Jack the Ripper isn't dead. This is crazy. I should call security to throw the lot of you out. I don't know why I'm not."

"Because you know deep down that we're telling the truth," Decker said. "You must have realized the absurdity of someone stealing the corpse. Nobody even knew it was there besides your own team and the coroner."

"And the corpse coming alive and strolling out on its own isn't more absurd?" Callie shook her head. "This is nuts. If the university finds out I'm even contemplating this, they'll withdraw my funding and fire me in a heartbeat. For goodness' sake, I'm a researcher, not a paranormal investigator."

"But you're keeping an open mind, which is good." Decker said. He turned to Stephanie. "What do you want to do with the watch?"

"I don't know." Stephanie picked up the fob watch and dropped it back into the box, then carefully replaced the lid. "My great-great-grandfather entrusted this to my family for a reason. To return the watch to the order of St. George if the Ripper ever reemerged. I've done that by handing it over to you." She pushed the box toward Decker.

"If that watch is important to Abraham Turner, he'll be looking for it," Colum said.

"Who's Abraham Turner," Callie asked, looking perplexed.

"If our research is correct, he's Jack the Ripper," Colum told her. "The name crops up in historical documents several times in relation to the house on Hay's Mews."

"Fascinating." Callie allowed herself to smile. "I can't decide if you're all insane, but you weave a good yarn."

"Are you going to take the box then?" Stephanie asked, fixing Decker with a hopeful stare. "I can't take it back. If the Ripper is out there and looking for it, it won't be safe at my house."

"Where have you been keeping it until now?" Colum asked. "It must have been secure."

"If you call a shoebox under my bed secure," Stephanie replied. "It's not like I have a bank vault tucked away behind the bathtub. I'm just a regular girl with a weird ancestor. At least, I thought he was weird until this week."

"The safe in the hotel room should be large enough to accommodate it," Decker said.

"Thank goodness." Stephanie gathered her bag and zipped up her coat. "I'm glad to get rid of it, to tell the truth."

"Are you kidding me?" Mina said. "Your great-great-grandfather was a kick ass monster Hunter, just like Decker here. Your family has been on a mission to protect the watch ever since. That's so cool."

"I'm glad someone thinks my crackpot family is cool," Stephanie said, but she couldn't help smiling as she started toward the door. "Now if you'll excuse me, I'd love to get out of this dank basement. I'm off home to crack open a bottle of wine and celebrate finally being free of that damned box."

# TWENTY-SIX

DECKER LED Mina and Colum back through the university building and out onto the quadrangle. They had left Callie in her office after borrowing a backpack within which to conceal the box containing the fob watch until they got it back to the hotel.

When they reached the road, Mina turned to Decker. "This is where I leave you. At least until tomorrow."

"Not so fast," Decker said. "I'm not letting you wander the streets at night with a killer on the loose. We are walking you back to your apartment."

"There's really no need," Mina protested. "I can take care of myself."

"I'm sure you can," Decker said. "That doesn't mean I'm going to let you."

Mina pulled a face.

"Come on, humor the man." Colum nudged her in the ribs. "Besides, you get to walk with the handsome Irishman for a while, so it's not all bad."

"You're full of yourself." Mina grinned. "I mean, handsome?"

"I think it's a fair description." Now Colum had a grin plastered on his face. "Rugged would work too."

"Knock it off, you two." Decker sighed. "You can flirt on your own time once we've dealt with Jack."

"We'd better do as he says," Colum said. "He gets cranky if people don't listen to him."

"Tell me about it," Mina laughed. She started off away from the quadrangle, then glanced back over her shoulder. "Come on then, chaperone me to my door like a pair of gentlemen."

They crossed the road and took a left, walking for a couple of minutes until they reached a four-story brick building with bay windows flanking a central entrance. A low brick wall topped with iron railings between pillars surrounded it. A light above the entrance bathed the path in yellow luminescence.

"This is me," Mina said. "Brinsley House. I'm on the second floor, the bay window on the right-hand side. It's nice. Quaint. You can come up if you want. I'm not supposed to have male visitors after nine, but I'm sure I can sneak you in. It's not like there's anyone around to enforce it or anything. Except my roommate, that is."

"I think walking you home will be good for tonight," Decker said. "Besides, I'd like to get to the hotel and phone Nancy."

"Say hi to her from me." Mina wrapped her arms around Decker and gave him a big hug. She released him and stepped toward the door. "I'll see you guys tomorrow."

"What, no hug for me?" Colum asked.

"You need to earn it first," Mina said, her cheeks reddening, just a little. Then, without waiting for his reply, she turned and walked into the building, giving a quick wave as she went before the door closed behind her.

"I think I'm making progress there," Colum said after she left.

Decker ignored the comment and started walking back toward the university. "Come on, let's go find a taxi."

"I think one may have found us," Colum said, nodding toward a car that was pulling up next to them, headlights blazing.

Decker turned to see a mint green VW Bug coming to a stop.

The window rolled down, and a familiar voice hailed them. "Do you chaps need a lift?"

# TWENTY-SEVEN

ABRAHAM WALKED through the dark streets. He could sense the watch calling to him, stronger than ever. He knew exactly where to go. The connection between himself and the stone disk hidden within the watch stretched back across the centuries. They were as inexorably linked as the Earth and Moon, and just like the Moon exerted its influence from afar, so the watch drew him ever closer.

He kept to the shadows; face turned away whenever he encountered an infrequent soul walking the same streets. In his pocket was the knife, one hand curled around the handle should he need it, but so far, he had not. No one challenged him, and the further he walked, keeping mainly to side streets and back alleys, the fewer people he encountered. It was while he was navigating one such alley, a narrow pathway between a builder's yard and a crumbling warehouse, that the signal from the watch faded once again.

Abraham stopped mid-stride. One minute he could feel the disk's energy, the next there was nothing except a vague connection, barely more than background noise. No matter, he could still sense the residual connection between them. It remained like a slowly dimming trail, leading him to the watch's last location. But he must hurry, or it might fade to nothing before he reached its terminus.

Abraham set off again, quicker this time. It took him another thirty minutes to arrive at his destination, a sprawling university campus that had grown exponentially since the last time he'd been in these parts. That was over a century ago, and although many of the buildings looked familiar, there were now other structures of glass and steel crowding in around them, robbing them of their majesty.

He hurried across an open grassed space with a fountain in the middle and soon found himself at an imposing Georgian building that rose three floors above the quadrangle. He mounted the steps and tried the main doors, only to find them locked. If he were at full strength, he could pry them open without issue, but as it was, he doubted his ability to succeed. The best way to get into the building, he decided, was to break a window. He descended the steps again and was about to go in search of a suitable entry point, when fate provided an easier way to access the building.

The main doors swung open, and three people exited. Two men and a woman. They were deep in conversation and didn't notice Abraham as he pressed himself back into the shadows under the building's eaves. They descended the steps and started across the quadrangle. He slipped out of his hiding place and up to the door, stopping it from closing moments before it clicked shut and locked him out again. He slipped inside and found himself in an expansive lobby with a staircase that ran up through the middle of the building.

The trail was growing cold now. His connection to the watch, which less than an hour ago had felt unbreakable, was dissipating like the early morning mist upon contact with the sun. But enough remained for him to follow, and rather than leading him up the ornate and wide staircase into the building proper, it took him downward into the bowels of the building via a concrete set of steps hidden behind the main stairs.

When he reached the bottom, he found himself in a long corridor. There were doors leading off on both sides, but he didn't want any of these. The door he wanted was at the end. He hurried toward it with single-minded intent.

He reached out and tried the handle. Unlocked.

He inched it open and peeked through. Shelves lined the room beyond, jammed with objects of all shapes and sizes. A desk and two chairs occupied the middle of the space, the former piled high with paperwork. There were boxes stacked in all corners. There was even an old gun leaning against a shelf. Abraham had once used a similar weapon, and he felt a tug of sentimentality, but it soon passed.

The room appeared to be empty. He pushed the door wider. The hinges squeaking in protest. He hesitated, but no one appeared, so he hurried inside, slipping past the door and closing it quickly behind him. He stood in the center of the room and glanced around, hoping to see his watch, but it was nowhere in sight. If only it was still calling to him, he could've walked straight to it, but as it was, he only knew that the watch had been here recently. Of its location now, he was clueless. That didn't mean it wasn't resting on one of the cluttered and overflowing shelves. He moved towards them, intent on searching each rack no matter how long it took. Even if he had to pull everything off. Except before he could even begin, Abraham heard footsteps from another room beyond the one in which he was currently standing.

He looked around for a place to conceal himself, found a gap between two racks and slid into the shadows within. His fingers curled around the knife and he took it out, just as a woman with wispy blond hair emerged from the back room.

Abraham lifted the knife and readied himself to step out from the shadows. He hadn't intended to kill again so soon, but he could see no other way. He must find his watch, and he couldn't search for it with this woman in the room. At least, not if she was still alive.

# TWENTY-EIGHT

THE VW BUG idled at the curb. Decker looked in through the window to see Stephanie Gleason behind the wheel. "Where are you going?" She asked.

"Back to our hotel," Decker said, recognizing Stephanie Gleason.

"Well, hop on in then, I'll give you a ride."

Decker looked at Colum, who shrugged. "Saves on the expense account."

"Very well then," Decker opened the passenger door and pushed the seat forward. "Who's going to take the back seat?"

"I believe it's your turn." Colum folded his arms and observed Decker. "You always get the front, and I'm bigger."

"You're not bigger, just wider." Decker climbed into the rear and pulled the seat back into position.

"Where are you staying?" Stephanie asked.

"The Reardon Grand," Colum told her.

"Hyde Park. Fancy." Stephanie swung the steering wheel to the right and pulled out. "Your organization must be well-funded."

Colum ignored the comment. "If you don't mind me asking, Miss Gleason, why are you here?"

"That's a good question," Decker said. "You left before we did. Were you following us?"

Stephanie hesitated before she spoke. "Okay. Yes, I was following you. But it's not how it looks. I wanted to talk to you in private, so I waited until you were alone. I didn't tell you everything about the watch. I know what Jack the Ripper needs it for. Or more accurately, why."

"I'm listening," Decker said.

"He wants the stone disk hidden inside."

"Why didn't you just tell us that when we were at the university?" Colum asked.

"I couldn't. My family is sworn to secrecy, only to discuss the matter with members of the Order. I had no choice but to include that researcher, Callie, in our initial discussion, since I had to go through her to get to you. But the less she knows, the better. For her own protection."

"Seems to me we've already told her plenty," Colum said.

"Which is why you're going to have to monitor her," Stephanie said. "Look, I didn't make the rules. I'm just following Thomas Finch's instructions. If you want to fill Callie in after I tell you what I know, then be my guest. It's out of my hands at that point. If something happens to her, it won't be because of me."

"This is all about satisfying your conscience then." Colum said. "Making sure you don't get blood on your hands."

"Not at all," Stephanie replied. "It's better if she doesn't know. Like you said, she could be in danger just by association."

"As could you," Decker said.

"I'm in no more danger than I ever was. I've been looking after the box for a decade since my father died. Jack could have come back at any point and sought me out. If anything, I'm safer now that you guys are on the scene."

"A fair assessment." Decker watched the dark streets of London slide by out of the car's side window. "We'll be at the hotel soon. If you have something to tell us, do it now."

"Of course." Stephanie took a deep breath. "Like I said, I know what the stone disk inside the watch is for. Jack, or rather Abraham Turner, can't extend his life without it. He must place the blood of a victim on the design carved into the stone, then hold the stone against the corresponding symbol burned into his wrist. As his victim dies, they transfer their life force to him. He gets all their remaining years. It also keeps him young and fresh. Reinvigorates him. I don't know how it works, some kind of demonic magic I suppose."

"Well, that's a pretty good reason to make sure he doesn't get his hands on it," Colum said.

"Because if he does, he would disappear into the general population and we'll never find him." Decker shuddered when he remembered the picture Callie had shown them. The wizened and mummified living corpse, still sitting in his chair. Right now, he would find it hard to move about freely because of his grotesque and memorable appearance, but if he rejuvenated himself, their job would get exponentially harder.

"There something else too. The watch in the box wasn't the only thing Thomas Finch passed down through the generations." They were whizzing along at a clip now. Stephanie weaved her way through the streets with the confidence of one who knew the city well. "Look in the glove box."

Colum did as she requested and found an orange padded envelope inside. He pulled it out. "What is this?"

"Look inside."

Colum opened the flap and reached in, pulling out a second, much older envelope. This one suffered from heavy foxing, the paper brown and mottled. "A letter?"

"Yes." Stephanie noted. They were approaching Hyde Park now. She slowed and turned onto Park Lane.

"What does it say?" Colum asked. He examined it briefly, then passed it back to Decker.

"I don't know for sure. The letter has remained sealed since Thomas Finch penned it back in 1889. But if I had to guess, I'd say it was advice on incapacitating the Ripper."

"A message from beyond the grave," Decker said.

"Precisely." Stephanie pulled up in front of the hotel. "You should wait until you reach your hotel rooms to open it. The instructions were quite explicit. Only you, as representatives of the Order, are to see its contents."

"In that case, we shall wait." Decker waited for Colum to open his door and climb out, then Decker followed suit. Before closing the door, he leaned back in and met Stephanie's gaze. "One more thing, Miss Gleason."

"Yes?"

"Where can we contact you, should we need to?"

"Here." Stephanie leaned across the passenger seat and offered Decker a business card.

"Thank you," Decker said. He glanced down at the card. "You're an architect."

"Yes. Residential mostly," Stephanie nodded. "If you're looking to add an extension to your semi-detached or build a She Shed, I'm your gal."

"I'll keep that in mind," Decker said. He reached into his pocket and took out one of his own cards. "Call me any time of day or night."

"I hope I won't need it," Stephanie said, accepting the card.

"Me too," Decker agreed, then he turned to follow Colum into the hotel.

# TWENTY-NINE

CALLIE WAS in the storage room behind her office browsing through the items they had taken from the Ripper's lair under the townhouse when she heard the office door open. She wondered if Decker and his companions were returning. Maybe they had changed their mind about keeping the box at the hotel.

She lifted the box of artifacts back onto the shelf and headed for the office, expecting to find someone waiting for her there, but when she entered the room, it was empty.

"Hello," Callie glanced around, surprised that she was alone. "Is anybody here?"

Only silence greeted her, interspersed with the rhythmic knock of the water pipes that ran in the ceiling above her head. She was so used to this sound that she hardly noticed it anymore.

She crossed to her desk and gathered up the folder containing the photos of Jack sitting lifeless in his den. She found it hard to believe he was alive. That a century-old corpse could have an ounce of life left within it was patently ludicrous. Dead people didn't get up and move around. Yet her recent visitors appeared to believe that was exactly what had happened. And not just Decker and his friends. Stephanie Gleason also accepted this version of events. Worse, they all seemed convinced that Jack's living corpse would come in search of his watch. An image ran through her mind of the desiccated and shriveled corpse staggering along the corridor toward her office, arms extended, and lips pressed back in a cruel grimace.

She shuddered.

"Get a grip on yourself, Callie," she muttered under her breath. She took the folder with the photos in it and opened her desk drawer, pushing them inside. As she did so, she noticed Jack's knife sitting there. She should lock it in the safe in the back room, where the most valuable artifacts were kept. But having the knife at hand made her feel more secure. If the zombified corpse of the Ripper really did stumble through her door, she would have something to protect herself with.

Not that it was likely to happen.

The more she thought about it, the more she concluded her recent visitors were nothing more than a bunch of deranged nut jobs, playing out some Ripperologist's fantasy. Even the box containing the fob watch proved nothing. The watch was a curiosity, for sure, but it was exactly what it looked like - an antique timepiece that someone had inexplicably put inside a lead-lined container. That didn't prove it had belonged to the Ripper, or that a living cadaver was searching for it. Not that she could explain the odd stone disk concealed within the watch, or why the emblem carved upon it matched the design on the Ripper's inside wrist. Maybe when they recovered the corpse, reanimated or not, they would get an answer to this riddle. But in the meantime, she was going home. She'd had enough for one day.

Callie closed the drawer and reached for her coat. She was about to lift it from the back of the chair when she caught a blur of motion from the corner of her eye. It was a subtle movement, a mere shifting of the shadows near the racks of shelves on the far wall.

She froze, her heart leaping into her mouth.

Maybe there was someone in here with her. She felt a knot of fear coil inside her stomach. The hairs stood up on the back of her neck. Then she realized how foolish she was being. She'd spent hundreds of hours down here at night and had never felt unsafe. The worst she'd ever seen were rats scurrying along the baseboards. Numerous complaints to university maintenance had done nothing to fix the problem, despite assurances to the contrary. She felt her heart rate slowing. It was probably just another hairy rodent foraging around, nothing more.

Even so, she couldn't shake the feeling of unease. She was afraid to look too closely into the shadows for what she might see there, so instead she scooped up her purse, rounded the desk, and hurried from the room, stopping only to lock the door behind her. It wasn't until she'd escaped the basement, hurried through the building's lobby, and exited onto the quadrangle, that she finally felt safe.

# THIRTY

ABRAHAM STOOD in the shadows and watched the blond-haired woman move about her office. He gripped the knife in his hand, ready to step out and neutralize her should it become necessary. At one point he thought she might have spotted him. She stopped and looked up from her desk, a nervous expression passing across her face. But then she took her purse and coat and hurried from the room. A moment later he heard the click of a deadbolt as she locked the door behind her.

Abraham was alone now.

He lingered a moment longer in the shadows, just to make sure that she would not return, and then stepped out and started his search. Floor-to-ceiling racks lined the walls, stuffed with objects. This would take a while. He began with the closest. The watch was not there. He moved to the next rack with the same result. The watch was small, but he could feel its trace energy lingering in the air like the afterglow of a dimming sunset. If it was here, he would find it. He was about to move on to another rack, when he heard footsteps approaching from the corridor.

He wondered if the woman was returning. He may have to use the knife after all. He crossed the room and slipped back into his hiding place. And not a moment too soon.

The door swung open.

He pushed flat against the wall just as a lanky kid with short curly hair stepped into the room.

The newcomer glanced around furtively, then hurried to the desk. He pulled the drawer open and reached in. When his hand came into view again, it gripped a knife.

Abraham's knife.

The one he'd used to kill his victims in the years before Abberline condemned him to a century of dark imprisonment. He'd assumed Abberline and his companion had taken the knife, along with everything else in Abraham's cellar. Now he realized his mistake. The knife had been there all along in that desk drawer, mere feet away, and he hadn't known. It took all his willpower not to step from between the racks right then and rip the kid open. Take the knife back. But he didn't. Because there was something about the way the young man held the knife in reverent awe. There was something else, too. Abraham recognized it in the man's eyes. Bloodlust.

This piqued Abraham's curiosity. Which was why, when the boy tucked the knife inside his coat and headed for the door, Abraham didn't stop him. Instead, he waited for the man to leave, locking the door behind him. Only then did Abraham slip from concealment. He approached the door and twisted the knob to pull back the deadbolt, then hurried after the kid.

He kept a suitable distance between them, staying out of sight, as he followed the young man through the building's lobby and then outside. From there, the kid led him away from the university, through a maze of narrow back streets. There were few people around and on the occasions the kid encountered a lone pedestrian, he crossed the road to avoid them and turned his face away. Abraham followed suit, keeping to the shadows and avoiding the yellow pools of light cast by the streetlamps.

After fifteen minutes, during which time they had moved far from the university, the kid turned onto a pathway toward a railroad bridge that crossed a set of tracks cut deep into the landscape, with steep embankments on each side. Here he paused, then veered from the path onto the overgrown verge. A building stood here. A raised brick structure that was once a signal box but had since fallen into disrepair and become the target of vandals. Graffiti covered its walls, abstract designs that overlapped each other with the freshest on top. The door lay half open on rusty hinges, an accumulation of dead leaves blown like a rotting snowdrift against its frame. The boy pushed through the unkempt grass and stopped toward the rear of the building, where he flattened himself out of sight. Abraham ducked from the path and found his own hiding place on the other side, stepping around a low wall behind which a copse of scraggly trees grew. He melted into the blackness between them, kicking aside an empty beer can that lay at his feet, and waited.

# THIRTY-ONE

DECKER WATCHED Stephanie Gleason's car pull away and drive off down Park Street before turning back to Colum. In his hand was the unopened letter she had given them moments earlier. A message across the decades from the Order of St. George and Thomas Finch.

"We should open that up and take a peek," Colum said. "I'm curious to see what our predecessor has to say."

"Agreed." Decker glanced down at the letter. "It's a testament to the dedication of Thomas Finch's descendants that they never gave in to temptation and opened this up before now."

Colum started toward the hotel's entrance. "We can read it in the bar if you like."

"No," Decker said. "I want to open it up in private. We'll do it in my room."

They crossed the hotel lobby toward the bank of elevators. A minute later they reached Decker's room.

Once they were inside Colum turned to Decker. "Let's do it then, I'm curious to see what that letter contains."

Decker nodded. He laid the fragile envelope on the hotel room's desk and pushed a fingernail under the flap. The ancient gum holding the envelope closed gave way easily, the flap coming up with no need to rip it open. Decker carefully withdrew the folded paper within and opened it up.

He read silently for a while.

"Well, what does it say?" Colum asked. "Come on, man, I'm bursting with curiosity here."

Decker continued reading but said nothing. He held up a finger, gesturing for Colum to wait. A moment later he folded the letter again, a thoughtful expression on his face.

"Tell me," Colum pressed. "Does it say anything useful?"

"It's more than useful." Decker turned the letter over in his hands. He looked troubled. "It tells us how to stop Abraham Turner."

"So, why the long face?" Colum asked.

"Here, read it for yourself." Decker held the letter out.

Colum reached out to take it, then hesitated. "Your demeanor tells me I might not like what's written on that sheet of paper."

"You are correct," Decker said. "In order for us to bring an end to Abraham Turner, someone will have to die by his hand."

# THIRTY-TWO

ABRAHAM TURNER STOOD in the darkness between the trees near the railroad tracks and waited to see what would happen next. On the other side of the narrow path, similarly concealed behind the crumbling and abandoned signal box, the young man also waited. The temperature had dropped during the evening hours and a chill wind tugged at Abraham's clothes and tussled what little hair still clung to his skull. Abraham didn't care. He'd weathered much colder climes. Once, many centuries ago, he'd camped near Hadrian's Wall for several days during a heavy snowfall, huddling together for warmth alongside the rest of his legion. Some froze to death, their fingers black with frostbite, faces blue. By the time battle commenced, their numbers had fallen by a third, and the rest were sluggish and stiff. All except Abraham and a few more of his kind. Such things didn't bother them.

Fifteen minutes passed.

Abraham began to wonder if anything was going to happen at all. He'd followed the man here out of curiosity, but now he was losing patience. It might serve him just as well to go over there, relieve the man of his life, and take his knife back.

But then he heard footsteps from the direction of the railway bridge.

Abraham edged forward and peered toward the bridge in time to see a slim woman, possibly in her late teens or perhaps her early twenties, crossing over toward them. She was a redhead; her shoulder length hair blowing out behind her as the stiff breeze tugged it. She wore a blue coat. Her legs were bare below a skimpy black skirt that ended at her thighs despite the nip that filled the air.

She was alone.

From the other side of the path, Abraham caught a flicker of movement. He was not the only one who had noticed the woman's approach. The young man had crept around to the side of the signal box, the knife clutched in his hand, raised and ready for use.

The woman was descending the steps as she came off the bridge, her heels clanging on the metal treads as she went. She reached the footpath and continued on, oblivious to the danger that lurked mere feet away. People were just as stupid now, Abraham mused, as they had been back in the glory days of his Whitechapel murders. No one ever thought it could happen to them.

The girl was level with the signal box now. She was walking at a good pace, a small handbag hanging from one shoulder.

The man who was lying in wait sensed his opportunity. He stepped out behind her onto the path.

She sensed the movement, made a half-turn, surprised.

The young man wrapped a quick arm around her waist, arresting her forward movement, and brought the knife to her neck with his other hand.

A startled grunt escaped her throat.

Abraham waited for the young woman's terrified scream. But her attacker moved too swiftly. He drew the knife across her throat before she could utter a sound.

Her eyes grew wide with shock as the knife bit deep, slicing through her neck and severing her windpipe.

He dragged her sideways, away from the path and into the dense undergrowth before pulling her to the side of the signal box. When he released her, she stumbled forward, her mouth opening and closing like a stricken fish hauled ashore. Then her legs gave way, and she flopped to the ground.

Abraham felt a surge of adrenaline as he watched the blood spill from the young woman's opened throat.

The man was standing over her, his own face flushed with delirium. He leaned down and wiped the knife's blade on the woman's skirt, then reached inside his coat and pulled out a white square of cloth. A handkerchief. As he did so a small rectangle of paper came away with it, unnoticed, and fluttered to the ground where it settled next to the woman's prone body.

The young man opened the handkerchief and wrapped the knife carefully within it, then inserted it back into his coat's inside pocket, before closing and zipping the coat up. He stood for a moment longer, observing his handiwork, then he stepped away from the woman and back onto the path, glancing cautiously around as he did so.

Abraham stepped backwards, letting the shadows swallow him up.

The man was on the move now. He pushed his hands into his pockets and sauntered off toward the railway bridge as if he had not a care in the world.

Abraham watched him climb the steps onto the bridge before slipping from his hiding place. As he passed by, he looked down at the young woman; her face already slack with death. Then he turned to follow the young man.

He ascended the steps and emerged onto the bridge. The man was near the other side of the span. Abraham followed as a train slid along the tracks in the darkness underneath, the rhythmic clack of its wheels drifting upward.

He reached the far side of the bridge and started down, then trailed the young man onto a residential street lined with terraced houses, their windows dark, occupants asleep by now no doubt. He felt a tingle of anticipation. The boy would be easy to subdue. But not yet. He would wait until the young man reached his destination. After that he would take his old knife back, and then he would find out what the kid knew about his watch.

# THIRTY-THREE

THE MORNING SUN had barely climbed above the horizon when Detective Inspector Elliot Mead got the call. Now he stood on the narrow path near the railway tracks and watched the Scene of a Crime Officer snapping photos of a body - a young woman clothed in a blue jacket and black miniskirt - sprawled among the weeds in the shadow of a crumbling signal box next to the footpath. The SOCO, wearing a light blue cover-all and mask, moved around the crime scene with the seasoned experience of one who has attended many such tragedies. A uniformed officer stood near the steps leading up onto a bridge. There would be another such officer on the other side of the bridge, preventing anyone from crossing over, partly to stop gawkers observing the scene, and also because there might be trace evidence on the bridge since it served as one of only two easy escape routes. This young man probably wished he'd drawn that duty instead. He looked positively green. He tried to avert his eyes from the horrific tableaux, but his gaze kept returning to the mutilated body.

"First time at a murder scene, mate?" Mead asked. He remembered his own initiation into the horrors of murder. A knifing in a Croydon back alley. A young man, staggering home from a Saturday night session in the local pub, dragged off the main thoroughfare and brutally beaten before a six-inch blade found his stomach. He'd died slowly, bleeding out mere feet away from a busy road but unable to summon help. A week later Mead's investigation team arrested four men, including a fourteen-year-old boy, all members of South London's Crow Boyz gang. He still thought about that senseless slaying when he was alone with his thoughts, even though he'd attended hundreds of gruesome crime scenes since.

"First time, yes," the constable nodded. "I've never even seen a dead body before this. At least, not like that…"

"How long have you been in the job?"

"A little over a year."

"It'll get easier," Mead said. "You mark my words."

"I hope so," The young constable dropped his gaze and stared down at the floor.

Mead turned his attention back to the job at hand. This was the third murder in a week. Three young women, all returning home late at night, all with their throats cut. And it all started the night they found Jack the Ripper's den underneath the house in Mayfair. In fact, the first murder was a mere stone's throw away from that location. Was there a connection? Mead couldn't see how there could be. The discovery of Jack's lair hadn't even made the papers until the next day. Yet the method of attack suggested a copycat killer. A deranged individual obsessed with the Whitechapel murders. Was someone trying to resurrect the fiend who'd stalked the darkened streets of London over a century before? Or was it just a random coincidence? A deranged serial killer with a similar modus operandi. Detective Inspector Mead didn't believe in coincidence. This was linked to the Ripper. He could sense it. Now all he had to do was find that link.

As it happened, he didn't have to wait long. The SOCO was kneeling now, examining the body close up. She paused, a pair of tweezers in her hand, and reached down.

"Sir?" She glanced in Mead's direction. "I think I have something here. You should see this."

Mead left the young constable guarding the bridge and ducked under the crime scene tape. The body looked worse close up. She lay with one leg twisted beneath her, arms at her sides as if she'd merely laid down in acceptance of her own demise. But her face told a different story. Her eyes were wide, staring sightlessly up at Mead as if imploring him to catch her killer. Her mouth was fixed in a tight grimace. But it was the vicious wound opening her neck that dispelled any notion this woman had succumbed easily to her fate. The attack had been vicious, the laceration deep. So much that it had cut through the cartilage around the windpipe before slicing and severing the carotid artery. It would have required a powerful arm to achieve such damage in one pass. Mead suspected the initial cut was more of a stabbing motion before the killer pulled the knife sideways. The copious amount of blood that spread around her like a sticky red blanket was proof enough that she had expired through exsanguination. How long she had been conscious, and if she'd seen her killer, was anyone's guess. Not that it mattered. Short of bringing in a medium, they would not be taking a statement from her. But that didn't mean she couldn't point them toward her assailant. Because the Scene of Crime Officer was plucking something out of the blood. A business card with handwriting on the back. It had been lying face down near the edge of the blood pool. Even though it was bloodstained, enough remained for Mead to read it.

"I did the best I could," she said. "We won't know what's on the front until we get this back to the lab, but the writing on the back is visible."

"Let me see." Detective Inspector Mead sank to one knee, careful to avoid the blood, and squinted at the card. There in a neat hand, was the first break of the case.

*Reardon Grand.*

*Room 803.*

"A hotel," the SOCO said.

"Fancy one at that," Mead replied. "It's on Park Lane. I took the wife to the restaurant there for our anniversary a couple of years ago. Not cheap."

"It looks like you'll be going back." The SOCO straightened up.

"Looks that way," Mead said. He doubted the victim dropped the card. It wouldn't have ended up atop a pool of her own blood if she had. That meant the killer must have lost it during the struggle. The occupant of the hotel room might have information vital to the investigation. Or, just as likely, they could be the killer.

# THIRTY-FOUR

DECKER AWOKE EARLY, having only gotten a few hours of solid sleep. His mind had been racing all night, digesting the information contained within Thomas Finch's letter. Not to mention the newly discovered information regarding the fob watch - now stashed in the room safe within its golden box - and the strange stone disk that it concealed. At 6 AM he gave up on the futile attempt at slumber and rose, dressing quickly and heading down to the lobby where he found that the coffee shop was already open. He purchased a croissant and a café au lait and took them both back to his room, where he consumed them while browsing the web on a company issued laptop that Adam Hunt had provided to him prior to their departure from Dublin. He searched for any historical record of Thomas Finch, but could find no mention of the man anywhere online. Of Jack the Ripper there was an abundance of information, although nothing that he found useful beyond the basic facts that almost everyone on the planet already knew. There was no mention of the man being apprehended and secretly walled up, or of a secret society called the Order of St. George. Not that he expected there to be. The predecessor to CUSP would surely have been as secretive as its modern counterpart. Even so he was a little surprised that there wasn't even a hint of a rumor regarding the organization. It was hard to maintain total secrecy. He was still pondering this when there was a knock at the door.

He closed the laptop and answered, expecting to find Colum waiting on the other side. Instead, a dark suited man he had never seen before stood in the hallway.

"John Decker?" The man said in a gruff, authoritative voice.

"Yes." Decker felt a tingle of unease. This man, dressed in a charcoal jacket and pressed trousers, tieless with his white shirt loose at the collar, might've been the hotel manager. But Decker didn't think so. His body language betrayed him. This was a cop.

When he spoke again, he confirmed Decker's suspicion. "My name is Detective Inspector Elliot Mead." He flashed a slim wallet with a warrant card inside then tucked it away again. "I wonder if I could trouble you for a few minutes of your time."

"May I ask why?" Decker inquired.

"Can I come in?" Mead asked. "Best not to conduct business in public."

"Sure." Decker shrugged and stepped aside, allowing the policeman entry into his room. After closing the door, he turned back to the man. "Would you mind answering my question?"

"How about you answer a few of mine." There was an edge in the detective inspector's voice.

"Fire away." Decker could see no point in obfuscating. He wondered why a British police officer, and a detective at that, was standing in his hotel room intent upon questioning him, but the quickest way to find out would be to let him continue.

"May I ask what your business is in London, sir?"

"I work for a research organization," Decker lied, utilizing the cover Adam Hunt had created for both himself and Colum. If anyone ran a background check their story would check out, at least long enough for them to complete their task unhindered. "We're collecting data on a recent discovery of historical importance not far from here."

"Jack the Ripper." Mead raised an eyebrow.

"Yes." Decker nodded. "That's right."

"I see. So, you would say that you have a vested interest in the subject."

"I'm not sure where this is going," Decker said. "We have all the required paperwork to be here and we haven't done anything wrong."

"How would you describe your interest in Jack the Ripper?" Mead asked.

"Our interest in the Ripper is purely academic," Decker replied. He could sense the detective inspector digging at something, dancing around the core issue. It was something he'd done himself during interrogations as a homicide detective with the NYPD. Ask the same question in different ways, hope your subject unwittingly tripped themselves up. Voluntary self-incrimination was hard to defend in court. "Can we get to the point, Detective Inspector Mead?"

"Very well." Mead glanced around the room, taking everything in. His eyes settled on the closed laptop. "You're an American."

"Yes." Decker resisted making the comment about the man's deductive skills.

"How long have you been in the country?"

"A few days."

"How many days would that be?" Mead asked. "Two, three? More than that?"

"We arrived the day before yesterday."

"Where were you before that?"

"Ireland."

"Was this trip to Ireland also for business?"

"Yes." Decker could feel the detective inspector circling around, looking for a way in.

"And what did you do there?" Mead asked. "In Ireland."

"I don't see how that's relevant."

"I'll decide what's relevant. Answer the question."

"I'm not in custody. I've broken no laws. I don't need to answer your questions." Decker was growing weary of the enigmatic questioning, which was surely linked to the Ripper, and the killings that had occurred since Abraham Turner's resurrection. Not that the detective inspector knew who he was really chasing. The man was clutching at straws, desperate for a lead, and somehow Decker had become the one he was currently grasping at. How the detective had even found him, Decker did not know. What he did know was that he wanted the man out of his hotel room. "I think we're done here, if you don't mind."

"I do mind, actually." The detective set his jaw and met Decker's gaze. "I have a suspicion you're not being totally honest with me. You know more than you're letting on. I'll ask you again, what was your business in Ireland?"

"And I'll say the same thing I did last time. It's not your concern."

"Very well," Mead said with a sigh. "If you're determined to make this hard."

Decker folded his arms and waited for what was about to transpire.

Mead went to the hotel room door and opened it. In the corridor beyond, two uniformed officers waited. He turned back to Decker. "I think we should finish this conversation elsewhere."

"Am I under arrest?" Decker asked.

"Not at all," Mead said. "But I would appreciate your cooperation."

"And if I refuse?"

"You *are* going to answer my questions. I assure you of that. It would be easier for both of us if you were to do so voluntarily."

"Come on then," Decker grabbed his jacket and headed for the door. "Let's get this over with."

# THIRTY-FIVE

MARTIN SLADE SAT on a chair from his dining room set, hands behind his back. He tried to move but couldn't. His wrists were bound to the chair with duct tape from a roll he kept in one of the kitchen drawers. His ankles were similarly restrained, one held against each chair leg. It had been a long night, during which Martin had passed out at least twice. Now, he sat helpless and scared in the middle of his own living room, clothes torn, face caked with dried blood from multiple lacerations. His captor had subdued him the previous night as Martin was unlocking his front door. He'd come up from behind, swift and silent, put a knife to Martin's throat. Then he'd taken the larger, deadlier blade hidden within Martin's coat. After that, things got weird. And even more frightening, if that was possible. His assailant was the missing corpse from the basement on Hay's Mews. How that could be, Martin had no idea, but he could not question the evidence of his own eyes. Martin was in the presence of the real Jack the Ripper. A man who should have been dead over a century ago. A walking corpse who now reclined on Martin's sofa and observed him with glowering eyes.

"This would go so much easier if you just told me what I want to know," the Ripper said in a raspy, thin voice. "Or I can just keep having fun with you."

"I can't tell you anything," Martin protested. He stifled a sob. "Please, just let me go."

"Like you let that young lady go free last night?"

"That was different."

"I understand." The Ripper nodded. "You want to be just like me."

"Maybe."

"I appreciate the sentiment. That won't happen though. You can never be like me. Not fully." The Ripper observed Martin with a cold stare. "I can do the next best thing though. Would you like to be the first person to know my true identity?"

"What?" Martin felt the knot of fear tighten in his stomach. He wondered if he would live through the day. "Why?"

"Because you took those handcuffs off me. You released me from a prison of interminable slumber. Call it a reward. Besides, I always wanted a prodigy. I must confess to feeling a measure of self-gratification, watching you dispatch that girl the way you did. I assume you killed the previous girl too."

Martin nodded.

"Most excellent. They say imitation is the sincerest form of flattery. You can consider me well and truly flattered."

"Are you going to kill me?"

"Would you like me to?"

"No. Of course not." Martin tugged at his restraints again, but it was no use. He blinked, trying to clear away the blood that had crusted around his eyes. "If you let me go now, I won't tell anyone about you. Honest I won't. I don't even know your name yet, so I couldn't, you see?"

"Abraham Turner."

"Oh please, no."

"Now you know my name, we're linked forever, you and I." Abraham stood and crossed to Martin. He let the knife trail across his throat. "Now, why don't you be a good boy and tell me what I want to know. Where is my watch?"

"I've told you already, I know nothing about a watch."

"I don't believe you. I sensed it in that room where I first saw you. You have my watch, or you know where it is."

"I swear, I really don't." Martin was shaking. He could feel the end of his life fast approaching. He was about to be murdered by the very man he had emulated with such glee. The irony was not lost on him. "Maybe the woman has it."

"What woman?" Abraham leaned in close. He placed the knife back against Martin's throat.

"She came to see us yesterday. She claimed to be the descendant of some guy who worked with Abberline of Scotland Yard."

"Abberline?"

"Yes." Martin could feel the knife pressing against his neck. He tried to move his head away from the blade.

"What did she want?"

"I don't know. My boss, Callie, spoke to her. I could call if you like, see if she knows about the watch. My phone's in my pocket."

"Phone?" Abraham looked puzzled. "You mean like Alexander Bell's device?"

"What?" It took a moment for Martin to understand. "Oh. Yes. Something like that."

"How can you have a telephone in your pocket?"

"They've come along since you were last around," Martin said. "I can show you, but I'll need my hands."

"You can have one hand." Abraham walked around to the back of the chair and sliced the tape. "But I warn you, double cross me, and this knife goes in your neck."

# THIRTY-SIX

THE DOOR WAS UNLOCKED and standing ajar when Callie Balfour arrived early at her basement office before the start of morning classes. This surprised her because she remembered locking it the previous night when she left. She hesitated, wondering if she should call security. John Decker told her to be careful, that the Ripper would come looking for the watch. Even now, hours after their conversation, she still found it hard to believe that the corpse in the basement on Hay's Mews had stood up and walked out of its own volition. It made no sense. She'd laid awake for hours thinking about it, watching the LED numbers on her clock radio count away the small hours. Eventually sleep came, but it was not restful. Her dreams were full of staggering, half-dead figures that chased her through London's empty streets as fog coiled around them and the screams of tortured souls echoed. She'd woken up with the sun, her body drenched in sweat. Unable to fall back to sleep, she'd given up and taken a shower, then drank two cups of coffee before heading out the door.

Now she was standing outside her office, images of the stumbling corpses that had haunted her dreams filling her head. Was there such a creature waiting inside her office? But of course not. She was letting her frazzled nerves get the better of her. She had probably just forgotten to lock the door the previous evening and was remembering her actions incorrectly.

She reached out a hand to push the door open, hesitating at the threshold anyway. When no zombified creatures lurched at her from the dark recesses of the room, Callie let out a relieved sigh. She stepped inside and closed the door behind her. Even so, she couldn't shake the nagging sense that she hadn't forgotten to lock up before she left. It was unlike her. There were many items of historical or monetary interest stored on her shelves, or in the room behind her office, and making sure everything was secure when she left at night had become a habit. She crossed through the office to the storage area, just to check everything was where it should be.

Satisfied that all was in order, she went to her desk and sat down. There was a stack of term papers she'd been trying to work through for a week, and the distraction of the Ripper's lair, coupled with the ongoing diversion of John Decker and his associates, had ensured she hadn't made a dent in them. She would like to have the papers graded before the next lecture. Her students had worked hard, and it was only fair. She took the first paper from the pile and started reading. She'd barely made it through the first paragraph, however, when the phone rang.

She glanced at the screen.

It was Martin Slade; her graduate assistant.

He wasn't due in until the afternoon. She wondered if he was looking to beg off work. He was a bright enough lad, but not the hardest worker. He'd also called in sick twice in the past when he was suffering from nothing more than a hangover. Still, what he lacked in industriousness he made up for in enthusiasm. Especially now he was working on the Ripper research. He practically begged her to take him along when they got the call to inspect the Whitechapel murderer's den. On the way there, in the car, he wouldn't stop talking about Jack the Ripper. He was, it appeared, a super fan. Although Callie didn't think fan was the right word. It made the Victorian murderer sound like a boy band. An obsession would be closer to the mark. He'd known everything about the elusive killer and recited a history lesson that included more than a few conspiracy theories and assumptions. She wondered if he'd sensed her disinterest in the more sensationalized aspects of the case. Callie preferred to stick to facts. Most of the information about Jack the Ripper was fantasy or conjecture. At least until they found that bricked up room.

The phone was still ringing, or rather vibrating its way across the table, because she had it set to silent.

She would never get these papers marked. It was a hopeless endeavor. With a scowl on her face, Callie picked up the handset before it buzzed itself onto the floor and answered.

# THIRTY-SEVEN

JOHN DECKER SAT in a small white room behind a table with a fake wood top and metal legs. A narrow oblong window, set high toward the ceiling, cast a slanting beam of weak daylight onto the opposite wall.

His chair was uncomfortable. He'd been here for almost an hour already and so far, no one had talked to him beyond instructions to sit tight. He was not under arrest, as far as he could gauge. The interview room's open door backed up this assumption. You didn't leave a suspect in an unlocked room if you'd read him his rights. The surveillance camera near the ceiling in the far corner of the room, however, served as a reminder that if he attempted to leave his freedom would be curtailed in short order.

Decker sat back and folded his arms. Colum would surely know he was missing by now. When DI Elliot Mead had showed up at the hotel, Decker hadn't mentioned his partner in the room next door. There was no point in both of them being dragged down to the police station. Not that Decker knew why he was here. The detective inspector had put him in this room and left without offering even a hint. It was about the Ripper and the recent murders. That much was obvious. The bigger question was how the detective had connected Decker to the Ripper.

They had stayed inconspicuous, and he was sure that neither Callie Balfour, nor Stephanie Gleason, had spoken to the local constabulary regarding his and Colum's activities. The only time they had come in contact with the police was on the night of their arrival when Colum had whipped out a fake warrant card to gain access to the alley opposite the Ripper's former abode. It was unlikely he'd pulled Decker in because of that. For a start, he wasn't the one who had impersonated a police officer. At least, not directly. So that left Decker wondering what this was all about.

He didn't need to wait long to find out.

The detective inspector strode through the doorway and took up residence in a chair across the table. Another police officer accompanied him, trailing a few feet behind. A woman, younger than Mead. Decker suspected she may be a junior detective, possibly not long out of uniform.

Mead reached over and turned on a recording device. A light on the front lit up red. He glanced at his watch, checked the time, and relayed it along with the date for the benefit of the recorder. After that he identified both himself and his companion by name and rank. Finally, he looked at Decker. "Would you mind speaking your name for the recording, sir?"

"John Decker."

Mead leaned forward. "Just to let you know, sir, the interview is being recorded."

Decker nodded. "This isn't my first time in an interview room."

"So I gather," Mead met Decker's gaze. "You worked as a homicide detective in New York."

"That's right."

"At least until you quit and took a job as a small-town sheriff in Louisiana. Quite a demotion. Then you lost that job too."

"You've done your homework." Decker wondered how much the detective knew about the events in Wolf Haven. He'd clearly run a background check, and possibly even telephoned the States. Had he spoken to internal affairs?

"I've done some digging," Mead said. "Fascinating stuff. Trouble seems to follow wherever you go."

Decker remained silent.

"You became disillusioned with the NYPD after a strange incident during which your partner tried to kill you."

"He was a troubled individual. He was also on the take."

"After that, you moved back to your old hometown and took a job running the sheriff's department. The same job your father had occupied before you."

"Is any of this relevant?" Decker asked.

"Just trying to get a handle on you. See what makes you tick." Mead rubbed his chin. "Your father's time as a sheriff in Wolf Haven didn't end very well, did it?"

"There's no reason to bring my father into this."

"Fair enough, but it didn't end well for you either, did it? I made a call to the Wolf Haven Sheriff's Department, spoke to the current sheriff. A man by the name of Chad Hardwick. I believe he was your former deputy?"

"That's right."

"You had quite a time of it, from what I hear. Sounds like you got yourself into a right mess."

"It's all in the past. I have a new life now."

"Ah, yes. You work for a research organization."

"Yes."

"I checked into that. Everything appears to be in order." Mead tapped the desk with one finger. "I don't get it though. You've worked in law enforcement all your life, and then you change jobs mid-career and go to work for a research organization?"

"I needed a change." Decker didn't know if the detective would believe him, and he didn't care. As long as his cover held no one could disprove his answer.

"And here you are investigating Jack the Ripper while there's a copycat killer running around killing people."

"I know nothing about any murders," Decker lied. "As I told you, my interest is historical. If you've checked up on me then you must surely have verified that I've only been in the country for two days."

"I confirmed your arrival through Heathrow," Mead said. He narrowed his eyes. "Your presence here still bothers me. I can't put my finger on it, but I know you're not telling me the whole truth."

Decker shrugged. The detective inspector had reached a dead end, and they both knew it. He was still in Ireland when the first murder took place, which ruled him out as a suspect. This tangle with the police would mean that he and Colum would have to be more careful in tracking the Ripper, but it was nothing they couldn't handle.

"You have nothing to say?" Mead asked.

"I'm not sure what I can say." Decker replied. "If you have a specific question, I'll answer it, but otherwise I believe I'm free to go."

"Very well. I do have one question, but you must excuse me for just a minute." Mead stood and went to the door. He exited, then came back less than a minute later carrying a clear plastic evidence bag. He retook his seat and put the bag on the table in front of Decker. "Perhaps you can explain this."

Decker looked down. Inside the bag was a bloodstained business card. On the back, written in his own hand, was his name and room number. "I'm not sure what you want me to say."

"Well, you can start by telling me who you gave it to," Mead said, pushing the evidence bag closer, "and how it ended up at the scene of a murder."

# THIRTY-EIGHT

CALLIE ANSWERED THE PHONE.

"Martin, you'd better not be calling to ask for the afternoon off," she said. "You've taken time off twice in the last month already. I'm snowed under with marking papers and I need someone to inventory the Ripper artifacts. I can't afford to have you out today."

"I'm not calling to beg off work," Martin said, quickly. There was an edge to his voice. "I'll do the inventory, don't worry about that. Speaking of the Ripper, I need to ask you about that woman, Stephanie Gleason, that came to see us yesterday. I've been doing some research, digging around on the Internet, and I need to know if she mentioned a watch."

"What kind of digging?" Callie asked. It was unlike her assistant to be so proactive, especially on his own time, and she wondered how he could've found out about the watch. Stephanie Gleason hadn't mentioned it in Martin's presence. The only other people who knew it existed were herself and John Decker's group, and she was sure he hadn't talked to them. "What makes you think the Ripper had a watch?"

Martin hesitated before he answered. "It's just something I came across online. A mention on one of the Ripper websites. I want to verify it, that's all."

Now it was Callie's turn to hesitate. Martin didn't sound like himself. "Martin, are you okay?"

"I'm fine. Did that woman mention a fob watch?"

"Yes. Her great-great-grandfather passed it down through her family," Callie replied. "Why?"

"Where's the watch now?" Martin's voice quickened. "Does she still have it?"

"No."

"Where is it then?" Martin asked. "Did she leave it with you?"

Callie was growing suspicious. "What's all this about, Martin?"

"Dammit, just answer the question. Do you have the watch or not?" Martin practically screamed down the phone.

Callie pulled the phone away from her ear, shocked. He was usually so quiet and timid. She placed the phone back to her ear. "Martin, I'm worried about you. What's going on?"

"I'm sorry," Martin's voice was returning to normal. "I shouldn't have shouted. I know that. It's just that…"

"Just what?"

"I want to come over and see the watch. If you have it, please tell me. It's important."

"You can't see it. The watch isn't here." Callie said. "John Decker has it."

"Decker?" There was a moment of silence on the other end of the line. "You mean those two guys we let into the Ripper's house? Mina's friends?"

"Yes," Callie replied. "They came here last night and met with Stephanie Gleason. Decker took it with him when they left."

"You're sure about that?"

"Martin, where is this going?" Callie asked. "You would tell me if there was something wrong, wouldn't you?"

"I'm fine," Martin replied. "I have to go."

"Martin, wait…" Callie said, but her assistant had already hung up. She sat there for a while, staring at the phone, wondering what had just happened. This was not the Martin that she knew. Why was he so obsessed with the watch? Come to that, how had he even known about it? It didn't make sense. Then she remembered her unease the previous evening, as if she were being watched. Was it possible that someone had been there in the room with her? Was Martin's odd behavior connected to her strange sense of disquiet?

She felt a prickle of fear.

It would have been okay though. The Ripper's knife was in her desk. If there had been someone in the room, she could have defended herself. She slid the desk drawer open to check the knife was still there. It wasn't. She searched the desk, picking up paperwork and moving it aside, but didn't find it. She sat back, perplexed. The knife was in her drawer when she put the photos away the previous evening. She hadn't moved it since. That could only mean one thing. Someone had taken it.

Now the fear was creeping its way up her spine, coiling upwards like a serpent. Even though she knew she was alone, she glanced around the room, nervous. And then she remembered what she'd told Martin. That John Decker had the watch. It might be an overreaction, but suddenly she didn't trust her assistant. She should warn Decker. She picked up her phone and dialed his number, then waited for it to connect.

There was no answer.

The call went to voicemail.

She left a message and then stood up, pushing the phone into her pocket. She would try again later. In the meantime, she didn't want to be in this dark basement room anymore. She grabbed her coat and headed for the door, fleeing her office for the second time in as many days.

# THIRTY-NINE

JOHN DECKER SAT in the interview room and wondered how much longer this would take. According to the clock on the wall, he had been here for a little over two hours already. Detective Inspector Mead had taken up a good amount of that time with his dogged questioning, which had become more intense once the detective had played his hand and shown Decker the bloody business card. This brought the number of killings that bore the hallmark of the Ripper to three. It was, Decker mused, lucky that he had been out of the country when the first slaying had taken place, or he might have found himself under arrest instead of being free, at least in spirit, to leave at any point. Not that Decker thought the police officer positioned at the interrogation room's open door would actually allow him to walk out.

As for the business card, Decker was clueless. He'd recognized it instantly as one of the two cards given to Callie Balfour and her assistant, Martin Slade, the previous afternoon when they inspected the Ripper's den under the townhouse on Hay's Mews. Decker couldn't imagine how it came to be in a pool of blood next to a girl with her throat cut, but the chilling conclusion was that either Callie or Martin had been present when the young woman lost her life. Since he and Colum, along with Mina, had spent the evening with Callie

Balfour and Stephanie Gleason at the university, it was unlikely to be the postdoctoral researcher. That only left Martin Slade, but why would he be there when Abraham Turner was committing his crime? It was unlikely they were working together, given the circumstances. That left only one option. The Ripper didn't commit all three murders. That led Decker to another conclusion. Martin Slade was not the mild-mannered research assistant he purported to be.

"You need to tell me who you gave your business cards to." Mead still sat across the table from Decker, the evidence bag sitting between them. "In particular, I need to know if you recognize this business card."

"I only gave two cards out," Decker said. At least if he pointed the detective toward Martin Slade it would take the heat off of him to pursue the more dangerous threat. "They both work for the university."

"And their names would be?"

"The first one is Callie Balfour. She's a postdoctoral researcher in the criminology department. She's leading the team examining Jack the Ripper's house." Decker folded his arms. "I don't believe she's involved in the killings though."

"And why is that?" Mead asked.

Decker knew he must be careful. If he mentioned that he and Callie were together the previous evening, that would put him right back in the crosshairs as an accomplice since either Callie or Martin must have been at the crime scene. It would be hard to deny he knew anything about the murders if he confessed to being with one of the potential suspects during the crime's window of time. He thought for a moment to compose a carefully crafted reply, but then a sharp knock on the interview room door saved him.

Decker lifted his gaze toward the door and saw a uniformed officer standing there.

Mead announced the interruption for the benefit of the interview tape and then turned the recording off before pushing his chair back and standing up. He went to the door and conversed in low tones with the Constable before turning back to Decker. "I need to step out of the room for a few minutes. I'll remind you that while you are technically here voluntarily, it would be in your best interest to remain until I return. You understand?"

"Crystal-clear," Decker said.

"While I'm gone, how about you search that memory of yours, see if you can jog anything else loose?"

"I'll do my best," Decker replied with the barest hint of frustration.

"You do that." Mead turned and left the room, patting the constable who stood guard over the door on the shoulder in a silent communication to watch the room.

Decker settled back and put his arms behind his head. He closed his eyes. Martin Slade was at the murder scene while the crime was being committed. It was the only logical conclusion given the location of the business card and the alibi he knew Callie Balfour possessed. While it was within the realm of possibility that she had rushed out and committed the murder the second he, Colum, and Mina had departed her office, it was not likely. In Decker's experience, the most obvious solution was normally the correct one. Martin Slade was a copycat killer. This made sense given what he now knew about Abraham Turner, who killed primarily to extend his own life and used the stone disk within the watch, which was currently in Decker's hotel room safe, to accomplish that feat. Without the means to steal the life force of his victims, there would be no reason for the Ripper to kill beyond the pure pleasure of doing so, and Decker already knew that self-gratification was not the Ripper's motive. Turner was a real living vampire, albeit an unusual one.

Decker wished he could discuss his conclusions with Colum, but alas, he had no means to contact him. Detective Inspector Mead had wasted no time in confiscating Decker's cell phone along with his hotel room key. He had no way to contact anyone, and nowhere to go if he left the police station. Instead, all he could do was wait and see how this all played out.

# FORTY

MARTIN SLADE HUNG up the phone and looked up into the face of the man who had held him captive for the past twelve hours. "There's a watch, alright. The woman who came to see us yesterday, Stephanie Gleason, brought it to the office at the university last night after I left for the day."

"I knew it was there. I sensed as much," Abraham said. He felt a surge of hope. With any luck, the watch would soon be in his grasp and then he could rejuvenate himself. He would shed his withered, corpse-like appearance and be whole once more. He would be handsome and strong. People wouldn't recoil in horror at the sight of him. Even better, he would add years to his life, extending it yet again past the boundaries of natural mortality. "I followed it there. That's how I found *you*. My accidental protégé."

"There's nothing accidental about it. I've worshiped you ever since I first heard stories about Jack the Ripper. I've read everything I could find. Visited all the crime scenes, what's left of them. I can't believe you're actually alive, and in my living room. I studied criminology because of you."

"You did more than that." Abraham reached out and cupped his hand around the young man's cheek. The boy trembled, but he did not flinch. "You took my knife and put it back to work."

"It wanted me to," Martin said, a flicker of hope in his eyes. "It was calling to me. It wanted to feel the slice of flesh under its blade again."

"No. It wanted to come back to me," Abraham said, his eyes blazing. "You were merely the delivery boy."

"No." Martin's voice rose in pitch. "We're the same, you and me. We're linked by blood."

"Foolish boy." Abraham's face wrinkled like old leather when he frowned. "You think we're the same? We're not. If only you knew what I truly am. How long I've lived."

"Then show me. Make me like you."

"I'm not so sure about that," Abraham said. "But I'll make you a deal. You help me get what I want, and I might set you free. Now tell me, who has my watch?"

"These people took it. They're from some kind of research organization. One of them is a big Irishman. The other one's American. His name is John Decker."

"And where can I find John Decker?"

"My coat. The inside pocket." Martin nodded toward the sofa where his jacket lay discarded. "There's a business card. Decker wrote his hotel and room number on it."

"Now we're getting somewhere." Abraham went to the coat and picked it up. He reached a hand inside, searching the pocket. It was empty. He checked the other pockets, just to make sure, but they were empty too. He turned back to Martin Slade. "It's not here."

"That's impossible. It must be there."

"Well, it's not."

"Let me check." There was desperation in Martin's voice.

"Are you questioning me?"

"No," Martin's eyes flew wide. "I just–"

"The pocket is empty. There's no card." Abraham threw the coat across the room. He glared at Martin. "Tell me why I should keep you alive."

"I..."

"That's what I thought." Abraham lifted the knife.

"Wait. There's another way," Martin said, the words running into each other in his fear. "There was a girl with them. Another American. I think she's over here on some kind of exchange program. I know her. We share a few classes at the university. She must know where John Decker is staying. Maybe she could even convince him to bring you the watch."

"A girl." Abraham rubbed his chin thoughtfully. This was too perfect. He might get his watch back and have a ready-made victim to boot. "Can you get her to come here?" he asked, a plan forming at the back of his mind.

"I can try." Martin still had the phone in his hand. "I'll need to go into the university's student database to find her phone number. Access is restricted to lecturers and staff, but I've watched Callie logon enough times. I know her username and password."

"Just do it," Abraham snapped. "And make it quick."

"I'll need my other hand free. I can't do anything while I'm still tied up like this."

"Fine." Abraham went behind the chair and sliced the tape binding Martin's other wrist. "But I'm warning you, if you try anything, I'll gut you like a fish before you even know what's happening."

"I know." Martin was tapping furiously on his phone. It took a few minutes, but then he let out an exclamation. "I've got her phone number. I can call her. What should I say?"

"You'll think of something. Just get her over here right now." Abraham held the knife up. "And after that, you can show me exactly how this wondrous new pocket telephone works. I would like to learn how to use it for myself."

"I'll show you. It's not hard."

"Excellent. But first, make your call."

"Okay. I'm doing it." Martin dialed the number and lifted the phone to his ear.

It rang.

Martin could feel his heart pounding against his ribs.

It rang again.

She wasn't answering. This was bad.

By the fourth ring, he was losing hope.

Then it stopped ringing. Martin swallowed hard. Was it going to voicemail?

But then a female voice came on the line. It was Mina. He breathed a sigh of relief and started to talk.

# FORTY-ONE

MINA HAD JUST STEPPED out of a lecture when the phone rang. She didn't recognize the number but answered anyway. Decker's number was on her phone already. It would come up on the caller ID, but she wondered if it might be Colum, the burly Irishman. She hoped so and felt a pang of disappointment when she didn't recognize the voice on the other end.

"Mina?"

"Yes." The caller sounded familiar, but she couldn't place him. "Can I help you?"

"It's Martin." There was a pause on the other end of the line than the voice spoke again. "Martin Slade. We met at the house on Hay's Mews."

"I remember. We share some classes together."

"Sociology, yes," Martin said. "I hope I'm not catching you at a bad time."

"No, not at all." Mina navigated the corridor, avoiding clusters of students. "How did you get my number?"

"Callie Balfour gave it to me. I've been working on a special project with her regarding the Ripper discovery. She suggested I call you. I know you have an interest in the Whitechapel murders, and I've made an astonishing discovery. I could use some help, to be honest. I know that your friend, John Decker, has been looking into the situation too. This might help him as well."

"What is it?" Mina asked. She felt a flutter of excitement. "What have you found?"

"It's hard to explain. Look, I really need a second pair of eyes on this. You'll understand when you see it. It really is quite unusual. Can you meest me?"

"My classes are over for the day. I was just about to head home. I can come down to the criminology department. I'm just across campus."

"I'm not at the university, I'm at my flat. It's not far off campus, a five-minute walk. Could you meet me here?"

"At your flat?"

"Yes. I know it's unusual, but I'm not hitting on you, honest. I could use your help, and I think it will be of benefit to your friends too. If what I found is true, it will rewrite the entire history of Jack the Ripper."

"I can come over for a little while." Mina was exiting the building now. She descended the steps and started across the quadrangle. If Martin Slade really had found something, she could take it to Decker. It might help them track the Ripper. "Why don't you text me your address and I'll come right over."

"Perfect. You won't regret this. In fact, I think we might make history." Martin sounded excited now. He was talking faster and faster. "I'll send my address now and see you soon, okay?"

"I'm coming, don't worry," Mina said, then hung up. She reached the road. A moment later she heard the ping of a text coming through. It was Martin's address. She set off in that direction. As she walked, she made a call to Decker, but it went to voicemail. She left a message telling him she was going to Martin Slade's flat. He'd made a discovery about the Ripper. She finished by saying that she would call back later.

It only took a few minutes to reach Martin's block of flats. She wondered if the doors would require a key card, like her own accommodation, but when she pulled on them, they opened. She stepped inside and hurried up to the third floor and Martin's flat. When she knocked, he called out from within.

"It's open, just come on in."

Mina pushed the door open and stepped inside, letting it close behind her. The flat was in darkness, the shades drawn to block out what little sunlight filtered through the cloud cover. There were no lights on.

"Hello?" A vague feeling of trepidation overcame her. Why would Martin be sitting in the dark? "Is there anybody here?"

"I'm in the living room." Martin's voice sounded feeble. Quiet.

She made her way down the hallway. There was a bedroom on one side, the bed unmade. On the opposite side of the hall was a tiny kitchen. An odor of spoiled food wafted out. Mina wrinkled her nose. Then she reached the living room at the end of the short corridor.

She stepped inside.

This room was darker than the others, and at first, she couldn't see Martin. She stopped and waited for her eyes to adjust to the gloom. Little by little, the darkness eased as her pupils dilated to let in more light. A shape swam into view, sitting in the middle of the space, unmoving. She blinked and took a step forward, then stopped.

It was Martin, bound to the chair with a gag stuffed into his mouth. He observed her with pleading eyes.

Mina froze, paralyzed by fear.

Then her instincts took over.

This was a trap.

She turned to run. But before she could reach the door, a shape stepped from the darkness, blocking her path. She veered to the side, tried to dodge the looming figure.

The shape drew closer. Mina glimpsed her attacker for the first time. A wraith thin man, his face aged beyond old. Mummified skin cracked and stretched taut over a sunken skull.

And his eyes.

They burned with unholy fire.

A scream lodged in Mina's throat. She sped up to slip past. He lunged forward, taloned fingers reaching out. Then, just when she thought she would make it, those dreadful claws took hold, closing around her shoulder, nails digging painfully into her flesh. She cried out and twisted to break free, but it was no use. Her captor's grip was too tight.

"You're coming with me." His voice was rasping and hollow, full of dust.

"No." Mina screamed. She tried to pull away and retreat into the room, but she could not break free. And then she was being swung around like a rag doll. Her head contacted the doorframe. A shock of pain jolted down her neck and into her spine as her skull bounced and hit the woodwork a second time. She tasted blood in her mouth. She tried to cry out but could feel herself slipping into unconsciousness. As she crumpled to the floor and the blackness closed in, Mina's last memory was Jack the Ripper standing over her prone body, knife in hand, with a satisfied look upon his face.

# FORTY-TWO

ANOTHER HOUR PASSED with Decker waiting alone in the interrogation room. At one point he stood up and paced back and forth, finally unable to take the uncomfortable chair any longer. He did not leave, however. An officer still guarded the door, observing him with cool detachment.

Decker was on his fifteenth lap of the room when Detective Inspector Mead finally returned.

He did not look happy. When he spoke, he sounded equally despondent. "I have no more questions. You're free to go."

"Just like that?" Decker raised an eyebrow.

"If it was up to me, you'd be in a cell right now reflecting on the answers you gave." Mead leaned against the door frame. "But it's not."

"I guess I should be grateful then."

"You must have friends in high places. Just what organization do you work for, anyway?"

"We've discussed this already." Colum stepped into the room. "That's above your pay grade."

"I was wondering when you'd get here," Decker said. "You took your time."

"Had to make some calls."

"Adam Hunt?"

"Yup. He was in a surprisingly forgiving mood, considering we're operating under the radar."

"How could he be otherwise," Decker said. "You and he were sharing a jail cell in Ireland not too long ago. You might still be there if I hadn't gotten you out."

"Hilarious," Colum said. "I guess this makes us even. Your arrest had one benefit. Detective Inspector Mead will help us from now on, if we need it."

"So we are clear, Mister Decker was never under arrest," Mead said. "He was merely helping with our inquiries and as such, was free to leave at any time."

"The officer on the door would beg to differ," Decker pointed out, meeting with the detective's gaze. "But no matter. There's no harm done. I would love to get my phone and hotel room key back now, if you don't mind."

"Here." Mead took the items out of his pocket and held them out to Decker. "My Super has instructed me to render you any necessary assistance, but I would hope it will be a two-way street. If you find anything that can help with my murder investigation, I would appreciate your cooperation."

"Naturally." Decker nodded and took his phone and room key.

"So you don't forget, I'll remind you that three young women are dead." Mead stepped away from the door. "I would like to make sure there isn't a fourth."

"We understand, Detective Inspector." Colum motioned to Decker. "Are you ready to go?"

"One moment." Decker was checking his phone.

"Problem?" Colum asked.

"I have two missed calls. One from Callie, and another from Mina. There's a message too." He listened to it then lowered the phone, a frown on his face. "We have a problem."

"What?" Colum's face wrinkled with concern.

"Mina. Callie's assistant, Martin, called her. He asked her to meet him at his flat. He claimed there was a breakthrough regarding the Ripper."

"Why is that problem?" Colum asked.

"Because I think he might be a killer. My business card ended up at a murder scene. It was the one I gave Martin." Decker felt a tingle of foreboding. "And he just lured Mina to his flat."

"We don't know for sure he's a murderer."

"We don't know that he's not," Decker countered. "I'm sure the first murder in the alley opposite Hays Mews was Abraham Turner. I have a hunch Martin Slade committed the other two. We know he has an interest in the Ripper. He could very well be a copycat."

Mead looked between the two men. "Who is Abraham Turner?"

"Abraham Turner is Jack the Ripper."

Mead's face changed from inquisitive to incredulous. "Like, the real Jack the Ripper?"

"Yes."

"From Victorian times."

Decker could see he was losing the detective. "It makes no sense, I know. But you're going to have to trust us on this. Our colleague is in imminent danger."

"How long ago did she call?" Colum asked.

"More than an hour." Decker swallowed hard. "If she went to Martin's flat, she's probably already there."

"Then we need to warn her." There was concern in Colum's voice.

"Agreed." Decker found her number on his call list. He waited as it rang, willing her to pick up.

But she didn't pick up. Instead, it went to voicemail.

"Dammit." Decker shook his head. "This is bad. There's no reason she wouldn't answer."

"Unless she can't," Colum said, his tone ominous. "We have to get to Martin Slade's flat right now."

"Except we don't know where he lives." Decker lifted the phone again. "I'm going to call Callie Balfour. She'll have his address."

"Good idea." Colum turned to Mead. "It looks like we're going to need your help after all. Can you get us a car? Preferably something with lights. We don't have time to sit in traffic."

"I'll see what I can do," Mead answered. "Wait here. I'll be back." He disappeared, leaving Colum and Decker alone.

Colum shifted his attention back to Decker. "Is it ringing?"

"Yes," Decker replied. "And we'd better pray she answers, because I have a feeling that Mina is in a lot of trouble. I just hope we're not too late."

# FORTY-THREE

DETECTIVE INSPECTOR ELLIOT MEAD steered the police car through London's heavy mid-afternoon traffic. Decker sat in the passenger seat, phone in hand. Callie's worried voice emanated from the speaker for all to hear.

"I shouldn't have told Martin that you had the watch," she said. "I thought it was odd that he was asking about it, but I never thought he'd do anything like this. I feel awful. If anything happens to Mina, it will be my fault."

"You weren't to know," Decker said. He looked out of the window, watching the buildings crawl by. They were moving at a frustratingly slow pace, even with the lights on. It was taking people too long to get out of their way. If only he hadn't been in an interrogation room without his phone, Decker could have answered Mina's call and told her not to go to Martin's flat alone. "I appreciate you finding his address for us."

"It's the least I can do." Callie's voice cracked. She sounded close to tears. "Do you really think Martin is a serial killer?"

"It looks that way," Decker replied. "We'll find out soon enough, though. I just hope he hasn't hurt Mina."

"He has the Ripper's knife. It was here last night when I left the office and it's gone now. The only person who could have taken it is Martin." Callie sounded miserable. "He's obsessed with Jack the Ripper. He practically begged me to let him catalog the items in the Ripper's den. I never thought his dark fixations would turn deadly."

"We don't know that they have yet." Decker hoped against hope that when they arrived at Martin's apartment, it would be a big misunderstanding and Mina would be safe and sound, pouring over some newly uncovered evidence. "Don't forget, the Ripper is out there too."

"That doesn't make me feel any better," Callie said. "Martin was asking about the watch. I never mentioned it to him, and I'm sure that no one else did. Likewise, I don't think he could have found out about it online. The only way he would have that knowledge is if he were actually working with the Ripper."

"Let's not jump to conclusions," Decker said, although he realized that she was right. "Just stay by your phone, and I'll call you when we find Mina."

"Please do," Callie said. "I'll be waiting."

Decker hung up and glanced backward toward Colum, who was in the back seat. "I wish we had some weapons to go in there with. I don't relish going into an unknown situation unarmed."

"Me either," Colum admitted. "But we don't have any choice. If we had access to the armory in the back of my Land Rover, I'd be happier."

"We'd have never gotten into England with those guns in the back."

"I don't see why not. The guns are in a specially shielded compartment. They don't show up on X-ray or metal detectors. No one has ever found it."

"It wasn't worth the risk," Decker said. "Besides, flying was quicker."

"Guns?" Mead shot Decker a sideways glance. "Do I want to know?"

"Probably not."

"I'm still finding it hard to believe Jack the Ripper isn't dead."

Mead kept his eyes on the road, but his face was a picture of incredulity.

"I know it sounds nuts, but it's the truth," Decker replied. They had briefed the detective inspector while they were standing outside the police station waiting for a constable to bring the car around. DI Mead had looked at them like they were crazy. But regardless of his sentiments, his orders were to assist. Mead probably didn't believe a word they told him, but it didn't matter. He would get his proof soon enough when they found Abraham Turner. In the meantime, all Decker cared about was ensuring Mina's safety.

They were approaching the university campus area now. The detective turned his lights and siren off. "So we don't announce our presence," he said as they turned onto the street that housed Martin Slade's student accommodation.

"Smart thinking," Decker said.

They pulled up to the curb a little way down the street and stopped. Decker opened his door and jumped out, eager to reach Mina. The others joined him and together they made their way to the block of flats and up to the third floor. When they got there, Martin Slade's door was ajar.

Decker and Colum exchanged looks.

Detective Inspector Mead reached out and pushed the door, letting it swing silently inward.

Darkness swathed the hallway beyond.

They hesitated, wondering if anyone would rush out of the gloom, but the coast was clear.

Decker took a tentative step across the threshold, looking at doorways to his right and left. One was a bedroom. It was empty. The other was a kitchen with pans stacked up in the sink. The air wafting out was malodorous and heavy.

Colum stepped in behind Decker, with the detective bringing up the rear.

The whole place was eerily quiet. Only the refrigerator's rhythmic hum broke the silence. Decker felt a knot of dread coiled in his stomach. Wordlessly, he motioned them forward with one hand, while holding his phone up with the other, ready to turn on the flashlight should he need to.

They moved past the kitchen and bedroom, toward a door at the end of the hallway. This was the living room. Like the rest of the flat, inky darkness lay like a heavy blanket over the room.

Decker advanced into the room, noting the heavy curtains drawn across the window to block out the light.

He saw a shape in the darkness, sitting in the middle of the room, unmoving.

His heart leaped into his throat.

He aimed his phone, praying that it would not reveal Mina's mutilated corpse, and turned on the flashlight.

# FORTY-FOUR

DECKER'S FLASHLIGHT lit up the room, and the corpse sitting on a hardback chair in its center. He braced himself, expecting to see Mina's dead body staring back at him, but when he saw the occupant of the chair, his thudding heart quieted. It was not her.

Instead, the lifeless body of Martin Slade sat slumped, head bent low on his chest. A deep crimson patch had spread across his shirt. His arms hung at his sides. Blood had run down them and now dripped on the floor with a steady tap. He was bound to the chair with duct tape, ankles and hands lashed tight. When Decker drew closer, he noticed a gag stuffed into the boy's mouth. He also saw the deep gash that opened his throat. Decker swung the flashlight around the room, hoping he wouldn't see another body. When he didn't find Mina, he felt a surge of relief. There was still hope.

"Detective Inspector Mead, it looks like you've found your killer," Colum said from somewhere behind Decker. "Or at least, you've found the one your superiors will believe. I bet if you get a forensics team in here, they'll match this creep to trace evidence from one or more of the crime scenes."

"Question is, who killed him?" Mead asked, moving closer to the body, and peering at it.

"Jack the Ripper," Decker said. "Or more precisely, Abraham Turner. Which means he has Mina."

"Or he killed her," Colum said. "I hate to say this, but she might already be dead."

"I don't believe that she is," Decker said, mainly because Mina being dead was too much for him to bear. "She isn't here, which means he must have taken her with him. Why would he do that if he just wanted to kill her? He could've done that here."

"Because he needs a victim in order to rejuvenate and extend his life." Colum turned away from the corpse. "At least if you believe what Thomas Finch's letter told us."

"Then she isn't dead yet," Decker said. "Don't forget, we have the watch. He can't steal her life energy without that stone disk contained within it."

"I hope you're right," Colum said. "And if you are, we should get back to the hotel. Mina knows that we took the watch. She knows it's in your hotel room safe."

"She won't tell him where it is," Decker said, but even as he spoke the words, he wasn't sure. What if the Ripper tortured her? How long could she hold out? Then he remembered her spunk back in Shackleton, Alaska. She was brave. Not only that, but she would understand that if Abraham Turner got ahold of the watch, she would be dead. Silence was her best hope. He looked at Colum with renewed resolve. "She won't talk, no matter what he does to her."

"You don't know that. She's just a girl."

"But she's tough," Decker said. "This isn't the first situation Mina's found herself in." Then, to himself, he thought, I hope it won't be her last. He took a deep breath and pulled himself together. "But you're right, we should go back to the hotel and make sure the watch is secure."

"Or we could go to that house on Hay's Mews," Colum said. "Maybe he took her there."

"He didn't," Decker replied. Abraham Turner was smarter than that. He wouldn't return to the one place they would know to look.

"He's out there somewhere, but he won't be anywhere obvious. He's not stupid."

"London is a big place," Mead interjected. "You could search for months and never find her. Years even."

"Then we go back to the hotel," Colum said, dejected. "And we hope to God that we can figure out a way to track him."

"I have a hunch we won't need to," Decker said. He turned his back on the corpse and walked toward the door. "We have the watch. He has Mina."

"You think he'll get in touch with us?" Colum asked.

"Why else would he take her?"

"You're still assuming she won't tell him where the watch is." Colum clearly did not share Decker's belief that Mina would not break. A haunted look passed across his face. "I've seen grown men, soldiers, crack under torture. Back in my ranger days."

"She won't crack," Decker said. He wondered if Abraham was hurting her as they spoke. The thought made him feel sick. "There's nothing more we can do here. She's gone. We should go back to the hotel and regroup."

"I'll call this in, then return to the station and get some eyes on the streets," Mead said. "Maybe we'll get lucky and a bobby will spot them. Do you have a photograph of her?"

"I'll text you one," said Decker. "And if Abraham Turner contacts us, I'll call you right away."

"And if he doesn't?" Colum asked.

"Then I'll kick down every door in London until I find her," Decker said, a grim expression on his face. "I only hope she'll still be alive when I do."

# FORTY-FIVE

AS DARKNESS FELL over the city John Decker stood at the hotel room window and watched London's twinkling lights turn on. Somewhere out in the vast metropolis was Mina, held captive by a ruthless killer who would stop at nothing to get the watch currently sitting in the hotel room safe.

After departing Martin Slade's flat near the university campus, Decker had bid a temporary goodbye to Detective Inspector Mead. The detective inspector headed back to the station while Colum and Decker returned to the hotel. The first thing Decker did was place a call to Adam Hunt. There were certain items he wished to procure in anticipation of a meeting with Abraham Turner. While none of the requested objects were impossible to source without Hunt's help, his involvement would speed things up exponentially.

Now, with that arranged, all they could do was wait. Colum paced back and forth, the inaction driving him insane. His first instinct was to rush out and search for Mina, but since neither of them had any clue where she might be, it was a pointless endeavor. As the detective inspector had pointed out, London was a big place. Mina could be anywhere, and finding her among a population of nine million people would be impossible.

So, they waited.

"Would you stop that, you're making me even more nervous than I already am," Decker said as Colum completed yet another lap of the small room.

"I need to be doing something," Colum replied. He glanced at Decker, who had turned from the window to observe him. "I don't know how you can be so calm."

"I'm far from calm. Terrified would be a better description," Decker replied. Ever since they discovered Martin Slade's battered corpse tied to a chair, a squirming ball of dread had installed itself in Decker's chest. It was all he could do not to jump up and punch the wall. But it would do no good. Unrestrained emotion would not save Mina. No matter how hard it was, Decker needed to keep a clear head. "Irrespective of my mood, the situation is currently out of our control. Expending unnecessary energy that we may need later will do no one any good. Mina is counting on us to find her. I intend to do that. In the meantime, my energy is best spent by reining in my fear and analyzing the situation with a cool head."

"And what are your analytical skills telling you?"

"You were an Army Ranger before joining CUSP," Decker said, "trained to assess the situation from all angles and act accordingly even when it went against your base instincts. This may not be a battlefield, but we're dealing with a cunning enemy who has the advantage on us. What's your training telling you we should do?"

"Wait for the enemy to reveal himself," Colum answered, finally coming to a halt, and facing Decker. "Let him come to us and then obtain the tactical advantage."

"Which is precisely what we must do. Today's turn of events has left us no choice."

"Except that we've been waiting in this hotel room for two hours and he hasn't contacted us." There was frustration printed all over Colum's face. "He must know we have the watch. Why hasn't he called?"

"He wants us to worry," Decker said. "The longer he leaves it, the more anxious we will become, and more likely to agree to his terms."

"He's letting us fry in our own grease," Colum said.

"Huh?" Decker shot the Irishman a confused look.

"Just something my mother used to say," Colum replied.

"Your mother had a strange turn of phrase, but it's an accurate analogy."

"Yeah, well, it's driving me insane."

"He'll contact us before the night is out. I'm sure of it," Decker said.

Then, as if to prove him right, the phone rang.

Mina's name appeared on the screen.

Decker picked it up and switched to the speaker. He looked at Colum. "It's him."

"Answer it." The Irishman looked more nervous than ever. "And don't antagonize the bastard."

"I have no intention of doing anything to put Mina in further danger," Decker said. He hesitated a moment to collect his wits, finger poised over the screen, then answered.

A rasping, dry voice emanated from the speaker. "To whom do I have the pleasure of speaking?"

"How about you introduce yourself first," Decker said. He felt a pang of disappointment that it wasn't Mina on the other end. Not that he expected it to be.

"I think you who know I am." There was a hollow chuckle. "I'll oblige you, regardless. My name is Abraham Turner."

"John Decker."

"Pleased to make your acquaintance, Mr. Decker. I assume you know why I'm placing this call to you?"

"I can guess." Decker clenched his fist, opened it, then clenched it again.

"I'm sure you can," Abraham said. "Tell me, have you found my unwitting accomplice yet?"

"I assume you're referring to Martin Slade?" Decker saw Colum's jaw tighten. The small talk was clearly frustrating him, but Decker did not want to push Turner. He was also curious to confirm some details that had been speculation until now. "I assume he was working with you."

"Only at the end. Before that he was merely following in my footsteps the way a lesser artist might copy an old master. There was talent there, but it was raw. Unfocused. I must confess to being flattered though."

"Not flattered enough to let him live."

"I gave him the ultimate gift. He was dispatched by the very person he adored. I'm sure he would thank me, if his windpipe were still intact," Abraham said. "Besides, he rendered me one last service in death."

"And what would that be?" Decker asked.

"Why to be a scapegoat, of course. The police of this era will want to catch their man. This way it works out for everyone. Mister Slade will achieve notoriety as the murderer of three women, while I walk off into the sunset."

"But he didn't kill all of them," Decker said. "You were responsible for one death, at least. What makes you think I'll allow you to walk anywhere?"

"It's true, I dispatched the first of them. But my protégé will take the blame, anyway. The police are just as lazy in this century, I am sure. They will lump my victims with his. And let's be honest, no one is going to believe the real Jack the Ripper is still around. It's all worked out rather perfectly."

"I believe it. So does my partner. I won't allow you to disappear so easily."

"Then I shall give you a piece of advice," Abraham said. "You should rethink your position. I've killed more people than you could comprehend. Chase me, and you shall join their ranks. I promise you that."

"Your threats don't scare me," Decker said.

"They should. Because my words are not a threat." Abraham drew in a rattling breath. "Now if we are done sparring, I should like to get down to business. You have something I desire. I have something you desire. Do I need to spell out where this is going, or can you figure it out on your own?"

"You want to exchange the watch for Mina."

"Very good." There was a dramatic pause at the other end of the line. "We shall meet in precisely one hour at the bandstand in Hyde Park. Bring the watch and come alone or the girl dies. Do you understand?"

"I understand. But I need to know that Mina is okay first."

"You think I've killed her already."

"I just want to make sure she's safe. Let me hear her voice and I'll bring what you want. If you refuse, you will never see the watch again."

"I know where you're staying. I could simply come there and take the watch."

"You might know my hotel, but you don't know which room I'm in. Besides, you'd never get here in time. It will only take me a few seconds with a hammer to smash your precious stone disk into a thousand pieces."

There was silence on the other end of the phone.

"That's right. I know about the disk. I know what you are, and I know why you need it. Now put Mina on the line or you will never see it in one piece again."

"Very well."

Decker heard rustling and a hushed conversation that he could not make out, then he heard a familiar voice.

"Decker," Mina's voice quivered. "I'm so sorry, I didn't mean to…"

"That's enough." The Ripper came back on the line. "You've heard her voice. Now do as I say. The bandstand. One hour or she dies."

"I'll be there," Decker said.

"Make sure you are," Abraham replied, then he hung up.

# FORTY-SIX

MINA SAT in an office chair with her hands lashed behind her back. She didn't know where she was, thanks to the blindfold wrapped tightly over her eyes. A headache throbbed behind her forehead, a lingering effect of the Ripper's violent attack that had rendered her unconscious at Martin Slade's flat. How she arrived at her current location, Mina was not sure. All Mina knew was that she was no longer in the flat and that she was a prisoner of the very man that John Decker was trying to stop.

He was not in the room at present, and for this she was thankful. He had taken her phone and left. She was now alone. After he left, she called out to see if anyone would answer.

She received no response.

Martin Slade was not here. She wondered if he was dead. If so, she felt little remorse. He had lured her to his home and delivered her directly into the hands of Jack the Ripper. She wondered if he had been working for Abraham Turner voluntarily, or if the Ripper coerced him. If it was the latter, then it was unlikely he had survived. The Ripper would not want to leave any witnesses. This would apply equally to her, a thought which sent a shiver of dread through her. A torrent of questions flooded her mind. How long would he keep her alive?

Where had he gone? And why did he take her cell phone? The biggest question of all was why she was not already dead?

She had no answers for any of them.

She knew one thing, though. If she stayed here, she was unlikely to survive for long. She pulled at the duct tape that bound her wrists and ankles, hoping to worm her way free while Abraham Turner was otherwise engaged. She felt the tape give a little, but not enough to make a difference. She let out a frustrated grunt and flopped in the chair. If she were going to escape, she would have to come up with a better plan. Except there wasn't time. Abraham Turner was coming back.

He entered the room and walked toward her. The next thing she knew, the phone was thrust up against her ear.

He talked to her in hushed tones. "Tell your friend, Decker, that you're okay. Let him hear your voice."

Her heart leaped. John Decker was on the other end of the phone line. At least she could apologize for allowing Turner to capture her. But before she'd even gotten a full sentence out, the Ripper snatched the phone away again.

He retreated and uttered an ultimatum down the phone, then he hung up. He approached her again and bent low, his mouth inches from her ear. She recoiled as he spoke, trying to avoid his breath, laced as it was with the stench of death.

Abraham Turner gave her no quarter. "You'd better hope that John Decker does as he's told, or you will join that young friend of yours on a mortuary slab before the night is done."

That answered one question. Martin Slade was dead, just as she suspected. She mustered all the courage she could and spoke. "He wasn't my friend."

"Just as well. The things he liked to do to girls your age…" Abraham Turner's voice trailed off, and the insinuation was worse than if he had elaborated.

Mina suppressed a shudder. It had been foolish of her to rush over to that flat. She was so eager to help, so excited to get some information for Decker, that she hadn't stopped to think. Now she was paying the price. "You're hardly a saint," she said through gritted teeth.

"So true. But at least I kill for a purpose," Abraham said, apparently taking no offense to her words. "And now, we have to leave our snug little hideout."

"Where are we going?" Mina asked.

"You'll see soon enough."

Mina felt hands at her face, skin like old sandpaper. She tried to pull away, but then felt the blindfold lifting. She closed her eyes against the sudden light, then opened them again slowly. Abraham stood nearby, a wicked-looking knife in his hand. She looked around, surprised. She recognized this place. She'd been here twice in as many days. This was Callie Balfour's office. Martin would have had a key. Abraham Turner must have used it to gain access. It made sense. The Ripper would not want to go too far with an unconscious girl. She wondered how he'd gotten her down here with no one noticing. There were always students around campus. Now she thought about it, Mina had a vague recollection of stumbling along in a dazed state. He hadn't rendered her unconscious then, merely stunned her. That she could remember little about the journey from Martin's flat to the office worried her. It was likely she was suffering from a concussion. The last thing she remembered clearly was Abraham slamming her head into the wall. After that, it was hazy.

"Come along," Abraham rounded the desk and dragged Mina to her feet.

"You want the watch. You're going to swap me for it," Mina said, with a flash of realization.

"What a smart girl you are." Abraham pushed her toward the door. "I'm going to give you a warning. We have a brief walk ahead of us. Behave yourself. Act naturally. If you don't, I'll gut you before you can even scream. Then, when I'm done with you, I will kill John Decker, slowly and painfully. Do I make myself clear?"

"Yes," Mina said, her voice small. She hoped he couldn't see her shaking. As they crossed the office she glanced around, praying that she wouldn't find Callie Balfour's dead body, but there was no sign of the researcher. With any luck, she had gone home for the day and never even knew they were here. Mina felt the knife's tip pushing into the small of her back. She drew in a long breath and tried to steady her nerves. "You needn't worry. I won't try to escape."

"Pleased to hear it," Abraham said as they reached the door. He steered her into the corridor beyond, one hand holding her shoulder, the other keeping the knife in place. "As long as you do as I say, you might live to see the dawn."

# FORTY-SEVEN

DECKER SAT at the hotel room's small desk. In front of him was the golden box that he'd removed from the safe. Inside was the fob watch that he would exchange for Mina less than sixty minutes from now.

"Do you think it's a good idea to give him the watch?" Colum asked. He sat on the edge of the bed, having grown tired of pacing, but looked no less stressed.

"I think it's a horrible idea." Decker rubbed his neck. He could feel the muscles in his shoulders tensing up. "But if we don't, he'll kill Mina."

"A rock and a hard place," Colum said, shaking his head. "You know the minute he gets his hands on that watch he'll disappear and we'll never find him. Worse, he'll start killing again."

"If Adam Hunt comes through, that won't happen." Decker glanced at the clock next to his bed. The time was slipping away too quickly and there was still no sign of the items he'd requested from his boss.

"And if he doesn't?"

"I don't even want to think about that." Decker reached out a hand and touched the box. It felt cool under his fingers. "Either way, we have to give him the watch. I'm not willing to let Mina die."

"This is a hell of a situation," Colum grumbled. He didn't look happy.

Decker shook his head but said nothing.

Silence filled the room, deafening in its intensity, and this was worse than the lapsed conversation. When a light knock came at the door, Decker jumped up, relieved to be doing something. He answered to find Detective Inspector Mead on the other side. In his hands was a sage green duffel bag.

"I was barely back at the nick when I got a call from your boss." Mead stepped into the room and kicked the door closed with the heel of his shoe. He walked to the bed and dropped the duffel upon it. "When I was told to assist you chaps, I never thought I'd have to go on a shopping spree. This stuff was hard to get."

"You got everything I needed though, right?" Decker asked.

"See for yourself," Mead replied. He unzipped the bag and reached inside, withdrawing a long black hard sided carrying case. He put this on the bed next to the bag and lifted two latches on the front of the case. Inside was a knife with an intricately worked scabbard and handle. It rested within a cradle of protective foam. When Mead reached down and removed it from the case, the knife glinted and shimmered. He pulled it from its sheath.

"Is that blade made of solid gold?" Colum asked, his eyes wide.

"It is and damned heavy too, I might add." Mead inspected the knife, then handed it to Decker. "I hope you know what you're doing."

"Me too." Decker took the knife and felt its heft.

"Where on earth did you find it?" Colum asked.

"The British Museum." Mead looked at the knife as if he wanted to snatch it back and lock it safely away. "Not a simple task, convincing them to part with it. Your boss, Adam Hunt, made a last-minute call to the head curator and saved the day. Whatever he said worked."

"He can be persuasive." Colum reached out and touched the blade. "How old is it?"

"Not as old as you might think. It's an electrotype copy of a Sumerian knife found at the Royal Cemetery of Ur in southern Iraq. The original is still in Baghdad. If it wasn't a copy, I don't think they'd have parted with it regardless of how many strings your boss pulled."

"It's still gold," Decker said. "It doesn't matter whether it's a copy. It will suit our purposes."

"Just don't lose it," Mead said. "The museum will not be happy if they don't get their knife back. I even had to sign it out. If it goes missing, I probably won't get a paycheck for the next five years."

"I won't lose it," Decker said. "But I can't guarantee it will be this clean when I'm done."

"Why do you need it, anyway?" Mead asked. "I mean, solid gold? Wouldn't a regular knife work just as well for whatever you have in mind?"

"It absolutely would not," Colum said. He went to the desk and picked up the envelope that Stephanie Gleason had given them. "Detective Inspector Abberline of Scotland Yard, and his associate, Thomas Finch sent this letter down through time. The pair of them subdued the Ripper back in 1889 and they used a specific method to do it."

"Abberline. Wow. Guy's a legend," Mead said. "Let me guess, that letter has something to do with your need for gold."

"It has everything to do with gold," Decker said, continuing on for Colum. "Abraham Turner is not an ordinary man. He is, for want of a better word, a vampire."

"That's ridiculous." Mead didn't look convinced. "I know you believe Jack the Ripper came back to life and is now running around the city, but I find the idea as preposterous now as I did when you told me about it earlier today. As far as I'm concerned, Martin Slade was a sicko with a Ripper fetish acting out his fantasies. He clearly had an accomplice, and that's who took your friend. There's nothing supernatural about it and if your boss hadn't intervened, I would be out looking for that accomplice right now. But please, do continue. I must admit to being curious."

"Very well." Decker drew in a long breath. "As I was saying, Abberline and Finch restrained Abraham Turner through the use of gold dust which they mixed with the blood of his last victim and put inside a pair of bellows, which they then used as a delivery system by blowing the dust onto him. It stunned Abraham long enough for them to shackle him with a set of golden handcuffs, also smeared with his victim's blood. After that they walled up him up and hoped no one would ever find him."

"Why did they need all that blood?" Mead asked.

"Turner was bound to his victims through their blood," Colum chipped in. "That's how he stole their life force. He used the amulet in the watch and smeared their blood on it, then absorbed the blood by placing the amulet against a symbol burned into his wrist. As they died, their energy would transfer to him, imbuing Turner with whatever years they had left. The gold interfered with the process and subdued him, so long as it came from the same victim."

"But why gold?" Mead asked.

"Because he's a vampire of sorts," Decker replied. "He might not wither and die at the touch of sunlight, but he is susceptible to it, which is why he prefers to move around at night. Gold is a heavy element formed when stars explode in a supernova." Decker placed the knife on the bed. "It is, for want of a better description, sunlight condensed and converted into metal. At such concentrations it has an immediate and incapacitating effect on him."

"How did they know all of this back in 1889?" Mead asked. "I can't imagine the astronomers of the time knew much about supernovas let alone the cosmic origin of gold."

"They didn't." Decker replied. "They merely knew, through folklore and rumor, that pure gold had an effect on such creatures."

"In the same way that silver bullets kill a werewolf," Mead said.

"Something like that."

"Couldn't you just use garlic? It would be a lot easier to get ahold of."

"I don't have a clue if garlic works on monsters such as Abraham Turner," Decker said. "But I know that gold has an effect, and I'm not willing to experiment when failure will surely result in my own demise."

"Fair enough," Mead said. He reached into the bag again and took out another box, this one smaller. "This is the other item you requested."

"Fantastic," Decker exclaimed. He took the box and opened it. Inside was a small flat disk that resembled a plastic tile.

"The GPS tracker," Colum said.

"I borrowed it from the drug squad," Mead said. "They use them to track consignments of narcotics. You can track it on your phone. I already sent you a link to the app."

"Perfect. We need to get this into the watch as quickly as possible." Decker crossed to the desk upon which sat the box containing the fob watch. "We must keep the watch in the box while we install the tracker, though. Otherwise Abraham Turner will sense that we have removed it. I don't know how, but he's telepathically linked to the watch, or more accurately, the disk inside it."

"We'd better get to it then," Colum said. "We don't have a lot of time. You need to get over to the park if we're going to save Mina."

"Agreed." Decker lifted the lid off the box and turned the fob watch over. He opened the back and slipped out the stone disk. "I hope the tracker fits, it's tight inside here."

"I hate to bring this up," Colum said. "But we have another problem too."

"What?" Decker glanced over his shoulder, then looked back and continued working on the watch.

"The letter. It said we need the blood of a victim for the gold to work. Someone has to die."

"I'm aware of that," Decker said. "But right now, all I care about is getting Mina back. We'll figure the rest out after that."

"That doesn't sound like much of a plan," Colum said.

"That's because it's not," Decker replied. The tracker was in place. He set the carved stone disk back inside and closed the watch. He put on his jacket, then tucked the knife into the inside pocket. It was time to save Mina.

# FORTY-EIGHT

THEY WALKED through the darkened streets. Mina first, and Abraham Turner in lockstep behind, with one hand on her shoulder. The knife was still at Mina's back, the point pressing painfully against her lower spine. Fleeing was out of the question. She would never escape before the knife slipped deep, and she had no doubts regarding her captor's ability to follow through on his threats. She kept her eyes forward and did not seek help from the few pedestrians they passed as they made their way off the university campus and toward Hyde Park. Mina didn't know the way, having only been in London for a short time. The Ripper, however, appeared to know the streets well and pushed them along at a fast clip. It surprised her, given his outward appearance, that Turner possessed the energy to travel so far on foot. She knew better than to underestimate him, though. The violence with which he had subdued her in Martin Slade's flat led her to believe that Abraham Turner possessed hidden depths of strength. It would be unwise to test him. Besides, Decker was out there and would surely have a plan to save her and vanquish Turner.

They were approaching the park now. It stretched out ahead of them, much darker than the surrounding streets. They made their way inside; the gloom swallowing them up. They were alone here. Only the forlorn hoot of an owl, and the distant sounds of traffic on the roads surrounding Hyde Park broke the eerie silence. Abraham steered them across open grassland between clusters of trees, their branches spreading out and blocking what little moonlight filtered from above. It was as if they had stepped out of the twenty-first century and into a time before the city had overtaken the surrounding landscape.

Mina found it unsettling, and not just because of the sudden solitude, but also because she shared it with a creature born of centuries old nightmares. Who knew what Abraham Turner had seen over his long life, how many unfortunate souls had perished so he may live on. It sent a shiver up her spine.

They were approaching a structure now. The bandstand. This was where Turner would exchange her for the watch. She wondered what time it was. Was Decker already here, unseen in the darkness, watching them? She hoped so. It made her feel less vulnerable.

"Your friend will be here soon," Abraham said. "When he arrives, make sure you behave yourself. Do as I say and don't cause trouble. My knife is eager for fresh blood."

"Decker will never let you live," Mina said in a moment of bravado. She had no intention of letting the Ripper know how scared she really was. "You might get the watch, but he'll hunt you down."

"What did I say about behaving yourself?" Abraham replied.

"Okay, I'm sorry," Mina said, squirming as the knife pushed harder against her back. She felt the point slip through the fabric of her blouse and pierce her skin. She let out a yelp. "That hurts."

"It's a pinprick. I could do far worse, believe me." Abraham relaxed his pressure on the knife.

"Fine, I believe you." Mina could feel a trickle of blood where the knife's tip had penetrated, but it hadn't pushed deep enough to do any actual damage. It ruined her blouse though, which was a shame, because she'd only bought it the week before in Covent Garden. Still, better a ripped top than a knife buried in her back. She tried not to move and stared out into the darkness, wondering how much longer this would take. Then, with a surge of relief, she saw John Decker walking toward them, the golden box clutched in his hands.

# FORTY-NINE

THE PARK WAS DESERTED. Night lay like a heavy cloak across the slip of pristine nature within London's tight and crowded streets. Ahead of him, appearing out of the gloom, was the bandstand. Waiting next to it were two figures, one tall, the other diminutive. He felt a surge of relief. Mina was here. A few more minutes and she would be free.

He stepped from the pathway and started across the grass. In his hand was the golden box with the fob watch inside. As he drew near Abraham Turner held up a hand.

"That's close enough." The Ripper moved out of the shadows and into the light cast by a nearby streetlamp, keeping Mina in front like a shield. One hand rested on her shoulder. The other was obscured behind her back, no doubt holding a knife.

"Mina, are you okay?" Decker asked.

"Yes. I think so." Mina sounded scared.

"Enough." Abraham moved his hand behind Mina's back, and she let out a small whimper. "Did you come alone as I asked?"

"Yes." Decker nodded. "I'm alone."

"Excellent." Abraham's face contorted into a vague impression of a smile. "What about my watch?"

Decker held the box aloft. "It's in here."

"Take it out so I can see it."

"Very well." Decker opened the lid, reached inside, and lifted the watch free. "See. I brought it just as you instructed. Now release the girl."

"What kind of fool do you take me for?" Abraham shook his head. "You can have the girl after I get the watch."

"That doesn't work for me."

"Well it works for me," Abraham said. "And I hold the position of power. I have a knife at your young friend's back. If you don't do as I say I shall use it."

"How do I know I can trust you?" Decker lowered the hand holding the watch and cupped the timepiece in his palm.

"You don't." Abraham's eyes never left the watch. "But what choice do you have?"

"Don't give him the watch," Mina said, writhing in the Ripper's grip. "If you do, he'll kill another innocent person."

"And if you don't, I'll kill your friend." The Ripper's eyes blazed. He tightened his grip on her shoulder, causing Mina to cry out. "It's not much of a choice, really. Risk the death of a stranger at some point in the future, or assure the death of this girl right here and now. To be honest, I would love to sink my knife up to the hilt into this brat. She's annoying."

"But you won't because you want the watch. If you kill Mina, you will never see it again." Decker felt the weight of his own knife, the golden blade under his jacket pressed against his chest. He wondered if there was time to rush the Ripper and use it on him before he hurt Mina. He knew there wasn't. Besides, the golden blade would be useless without the blood of a victim. Attacking Abraham would probably condemn both himself and Mina to death. A surge of frustration welled inside Decker. Abraham held the advantage, and he knew it.

"Enough talk," Abraham said. "The watch. Give it to me."

"Come and take it," Decker said. He held his hand out and opened his fist to reveal the watch.

"I don't think so." Abraham didn't move. "Put the watch on the ground and step away."

"If I do that, you will release Mina?" Decker asked. He didn't trust Abraham, but he was in no position to argue.

"Of course." Abraham nodded. "I gave you my word, didn't I?"

"I'm not sure your word is worth much."

"We've been over this already. You don't trust me, and I don't trust you," Abraham said. "It's simple, really. You can put the watch on the ground and back off, or you can keep it and I'll kill Mina. Those are the two options. Make your choice quickly. My patience is running thin."

"I'll do as you say." Decker kneeled and reluctantly placed the watch on the grass. He stood, the golden box still under one arm, and took a couple of steps backward.

"Move further away if you please. Twenty feet should do it."

Decker complied. He stepped off the required distance, walking backwards and never taking his eyes off of Abraham Turner and Mina. When he was far enough away, the Ripper moved toward the watch, steering Mina in front of him. As he drew close he told her to pick it up. As he did so Decker caught sight of the blade at her back. He recognized it as the knife missing from Callie Balfour's office. No doubt Martin Slade had stolen it. Then the Ripper killed him and took it back.

Mina straightened up and allowed Abraham to take the watch from her.

"I've completed my part of the bargain, now you need to complete yours," Decker said. "Release Mina."

"You are correct, of course. You completed your part of the deal. You brought me my watch and for that I am eternally grateful."

"Then let her go," Decker said. He felt a shiver of foreboding crawl up his spine. There was something about the way Abraham Turner spoke that set his nerves jangling.

"How about I do you one better," Abraham said, the twisted smile returning to his face.

"What do you mean?" Decker asked, the foreboding flaring into full-blown panic.

"I'll release her soul instead," Abraham said.

Then, before Decker could react, the Ripper brought the knife around and plunged it deep into Mina's chest.

# FIFTY

"NO!" Decker's horrified scream rent the air.

Abraham pulled the knife free of Mina's chest and released her, then turned, watch in hand, and fled into the Stygian darkness.

Decker dropped the box and sprinted forward, arriving at Mina's location moments after she slumped to the ground. He slid down beside her and put his hand under her head. She looked up at him, her eyes wide with disbelief that swiftly turned to choking fear. Her breath came in wheezing gasps and when she talked, her voice was weak.

"I'm sorry," Mina said, each word and effort. "This is all my fault."

"Don't talk," Decker said. He could feel his eyes tearing up. A lump caught in his throat. "Save your strength."

Mina's eyelids fluttered, and he thought she might lose consciousness, but then she opened them again and looked up into his face. Her eyes made contact with his and Decker was disheartened to see the light dimming in them already.

Mina was dying.

He pulled her jacket back. There was less blood than he would have expected. The knife wound was clearly visible, a puckered and angry two inch slit just above her left breast. Her white blouse, now torn, was already soaking up whatever blood oozed from the wound. It reminded him of another piece of bloodied fabric he'd once seen, the shroud that covered his mother's torn and mutilated body as she lay in the morgue when he was a child. He hadn't been meant to see that. He'd peeked through the mostly closed door as his father talked to the coroner. He wished he weren't seeing this either. He had failed Mina. After promising to keep her safe, he had achieved the exact opposite. Now her demise would follow him for the rest of his days.

He glanced upward, into the night sky, a sob escaping his lips. Then he took a deep breath, took his phone out, and called Colum. He knew that every second he spent tending Mina was more time for the Ripper to make his escape. Even with the GPS tracker inside the watch, there was no guarantee that Decker could catch him, let alone vanquish him. But he didn't care. Right now his only concern was the young woman gasping for breath in his arms.

"Decker." Colum's voice blurted out the phone's speaker. "Is it done? Do you have Mina?"

"I have her," Decker said. "But it's not good. Tell Detective Inspector Mead to phone for an ambulance. His call might get them here faster."

"What's happened?" There was fear in Colum's voice. "Are you hurt?"

"Not me, Mina." Decker could hear the detective inspector talking in the background, summoning help. "He stabbed her."

"What?" Colum sounded shocked. "I knew we couldn't trust him. How bad is it?"

"It's pretty bad," Decker said. "Chest wound. The knife went pretty deep."

"I'm coming to you," Colum said. "We both are."

"You'd better get here quickly," Decker said. "I don't know how much time there is."

"Just keep her alive," Colum said. "We are on our way."

"I'm at the bandstand," Decker said. He heard rustling and then a door slam as Colum exited the hotel room. Mead was still talking, but he appeared to have hung up the phone and was conversing with Colum.

"The ambulance is on its way," Colum said at length. "We're in the lobby, leaving the hotel now."

Decker didn't reply. There was nothing to say. He dropped his phone onto the grass and looked down at Mina. There was more blood now, and her breathing was shallow. When he spoke to her. She didn't respond. He lifted his head and looked into the darkness where Abraham Turner had fled, and in that moment, he vowed to have his revenge.

# FIFTY-ONE

AFTER ABRAHAM TURNER thrust the knife into Mina's chest he turned and strode off into the darkness. Behind him, Decker's plaintive cry of horror drifted on the breeze. This brought a smile to Abraham's face. He could hardly believe that recovering his watch had been so easy. People in this century were so naïve. With the girl bleeding out from his knife wound, Abraham would have plenty of time to complete his escape. He had expected some trickery from John Decker but had seen no sign of it. The man had been as good as his word and had come to the park alone and apparently unarmed.

Abraham was at the edge of the park now. He slowed his frantic pace and allowed himself to look down at the watch. Finally, he could rejuvenate. He would shed his hideous appearance and look like everyone else. He would also extend his life by decades into the bargain. He turned the watch over and lifted the back. There, nestled inside, was the stone tablet. It was old, more ancient than even Abraham. He remembered the centuries it had laid around his neck, nestled next to his skin. Then, in Victorian times, he'd put it inside the watch. It was safer there, at least until Detective Inspector Abberline and his crony had found him on that cold winter night in 1889. They walled him up and left him for dead, then stole the watch. They must have thought it was the perfect insurance policy. Without the watch, he could not live on, even if he escaped his prison. But their scheming was all for naught.

They had failed.

Abraham had triumphed, just as he always did, and now he had the watch once more. He also had his knife back. Best of all, he was free to wreak havoc on this new and wonderful age. But first he must put as much distance between himself and John Decker as he could. The man might be too trusting, but he was no fool. Abraham closed the back of the watch and slipped it into his pocket. Then he turned and walked a little way along the pavement, his eyes upon the road.

Soon he saw what he was looking for.

A car, its headlights piercing the night.

Abraham concealed the knife behind his back and stepped out in its path.

He faced the oncoming vehicle and raised an arm.

The car came to a sudden halt with a screech of brakes. Abraham pulled the passenger side door open and climbed in. The lone occupant was a woman in her early forties. She let out a terrified screech and clawed at the driver's side door to escape. Except that in her panic, she forgot to unbuckle her seatbelt. Abraham reached over and grabbed her hair. He yanked her toward him, the motion violent and quick. Then he showed her the knife and told her to drive.

# FIFTY-TWO

DECKER WAS STILL CRADLING Mina's head when Colum and Detective Inspector Mead arrived. The Irishman took one look at her and dropped to his knees.

"How could this happen?" He asked, looking at Decker with questioning eyes.

"Because I let it," Decker said. "There was no way Turner was ever going to release Mina. Not alive anyway. I should never have given him the watch."

"You did what you thought was best." Colum took Mina's hand. Her eyes shifted from Decker, but they were unfocused.

Mead touched Decker on the shoulder. "There's an ambulance on the way."

As if to prove his words, the wail of sirens rose through the night. Decker glanced around and saw strobing blue lights across the park. They were getting closer. Moments from now help would be here. Decker felt a surge of relief.

"You need to go after Abraham," Colum said. He reached out a hand and moved Decker's own arm gently away from Mina's wound. "I'll keep the pressure on this, you deal with the bastard."

"I don't want to leave her like this," Decker said.

"You don't have any choice. If you don't stop him, Abraham Turner will keep killing."

"Go." Mina, who had been slipping in and out of consciousness, was momentarily alert. She raised a hand, the movement clearly a struggle. She touched Decker's face, then let the hand drop back to her side. "I'll be fine. It's barely a scratch."

"Mina…" Decker struggled to find the right words. A tear rolled down his cheek. "I'm afraid I'll never see you again."

"You're not that lucky," Mina said and even through her pain she managed a weak smile. She coughed. A thin line of blood appeared at the corner of her mouth and meandered along her jaw. "Finish him. I'll wait for you."

Decker glanced at Colum.

The big Irishman motioned for Decker to leave with a tilt of his head, but said nothing.

Decker stood up. Mina looked small and fragile laying on the grass. Like a broken doll. Her face was deathly white, and her eyes were losing focus once more. He stepped away, not wanting to see her like that.

"Wait." Colum looked up. "Give me the knife. You need the blood of a victim."

Decker reached into his coat and removed the knife. He handed it to Colum.

The Irishman drew the blade from its scabbard and touched his hand to it, transferring Mina's blood, then he slipped it back into its housing and held it out for Decker to take. "I hope this works."

"Me too," Decker said. Thomas Finch's instructions pushed their way into his mind. For the gold to affect Abraham Turner, the victim had to die.

The ambulance was pulling up now. Two men in fluorescent green and white jackets jumped out and rushed toward them.

Decker pushed the grim thought away and turned to Mead, slipping the sheathed knife back into his coat as he did so. "I'm going to need your car."

"Not bloody likely," Mead said. "Have you ever even driven on the left before?"

"It can't be that hard. I'll figure it out." Decker held out a hand. "Keys."

"Not going to happen," Mead said. "There are a lot of things I'll do, but handing over a police car to a civilian is not one of them. I'm coming with you."

"No, you're not." Decker glared at the detective. "It's too dangerous. Give me the keys. We're wasting time."

"Do I need to remind you I'm a police officer?" Mead asked. "I'm coming. Take it or leave it."

"I don't have time for this." Decker shook his head. "Just stay out of my way when we find Abraham Turner."

"Why don't we play that one by ear," Mead said.

"Fine." Decker glanced down at Mina. The paramedics were working on her, conversing in grave tones. It didn't look good.

Colum sat on the grass, his hands bloodied, and watched. Then he looked up at Decker. "I'll stay with her, I promise. I won't leave her side."

"I know." Decker took his phone out and started the GPS tracking app. Abraham Turner was already miles away. Decker wondered how he could have covered so much ground considering Turner had fled on foot. He had a feeling he wasn't going to like the answer. He took one last look at Mina. Would he ever see her alive again? Unwilling to contemplate his dire odds, he turned to Mead. "Let's go. We've got a killer to stop."

# FIFTY-THREE

THEY DROVE with the light bar activated but no siren. On the few occasions where a vehicle was slow to move aside, Mead leaned hard on the horn. The signal from the GPS tracker was stationary. It had stopped a few minutes after they left Hyde Park, which meant Abraham Turner had reached his destination. Decker kept his eyes on the screen as they closed in and gave Mead terse directions.

"I'm sorry about your friend," Mead said eventually, breaking the silence.

"Yeah." Decker stared ahead. That Mead hadn't offered encouragement could only mean one thing. He didn't think she was going to survive. To be honest, neither did Decker. The wound was too deep. Even if the knife had missed her heart, it had surely punctured a lung. If Mina wasn't dead already she was on borrowed time. He blinked back the tears that threatened to flow and tore his mind away from the dreadful scene they had just departed. He could not afford sentimentality right now. They were approaching Abraham Turner's position. According to the tracker, they were right on top of it. Decker glanced around as the detective inspector killed the light bar and edged down a neighborhood high street with small terraced shops to the left and right. This was the kind of community shopping that had long ago perished in many parts of the United States, replaced by megastores and chains in dreary strip malls. But here, in the heart of London, it thrived. There was a neighborhood bakery. An Italian restaurant. A barber's shop. When they reached a fish and chip shop tucked between a betting office and a bank, the app told them they had reached the end of the trail.

Mead pulled over. He peered through the car's side window. "It doesn't look open."

"It's late. Maybe they shut up shop for the night," Decker said, observing the darkened interior.

"I don't think so," Mead replied. "There's a sign on the door. Closed until further notice."

"The tracker says this is the spot." Decker glanced up toward the second floor. "There's a light on up there, so someone's home."

"Or they went on holiday and forgot to turn it off."

"He's here, I can feel it." Decker tore his eyes away from the window. "Let's look around before we go barging in. There's a road up here on the right. There might be a back entrance. I don't want him escaping again."

"Let's take a gander," Mead said, easing the car away from the curb and steering toward the side street a couple of storefronts distant before turning.

They were on a residential street now. Victorian terraced houses with thrusting bay windows lined both sides. But on the right, before the residential buildings began, was an access road. Mead turned in. There were no streetlamps, but his lights flared against the opposing building's walls as they edged forward. A little way down, next to a cluster of wheelie bins, sat a red Ford Fiesta parked at an angle that provided no room to pass.

Mead slowed to a crawl and advanced upon the abandoned vehicle. "This doesn't look good."

"There's someone inside," Decker said. Through the side window, he could see a shape sitting in the driver's seat. Whoever occupied the car did not acknowledge their approach.

Mead brought the police car to a stop behind the Ford. "Let's take a look."

Decker nodded. He opened his door and climbed out, then closed the door as softly as possible. They were directly behind the fish and chip shop. He could see the restaurant's name stenciled on a service door. Together, the two men approached the car the occupant still hadn't moved.

Decker leaned down and peered into the cabin. The driver was a middle-aged woman wearing a floral dress. She sat stiff and upright with her head slumped forward a little. Blood soaked the front of her dress. Decker straightened up and looked at Mead. "She's dead. He cut her throat."

"Just like the others," the detective said. "I was hoping the murders would've stopped with Martin Slade's death."

"Slade was just a fan boy." Decker went around to the other side of the car and opened up the driver's door. "The real monster is still alive."

"And in that chip shop, apparently." Mead glanced up towards the building.

"He's taken two victims tonight." Decker drew the Sumerian knife from his jacket and slid it from its sheath. Mina's dried blood caked the blade. Was she already dead? Decker felt his throat tighten.

"What are you doing?" Mead lingered impatiently toward the back of the vehicle.

"Insurance," Decker said. He placed the knife against the dead woman's throat, transferred a good amount of blood to the blade. That done he slid it into the scabbard once more and tucked it back into his jacket. "The blood of a victim. I don't know Mina is dead yet, but this poor woman is. The least she can do is provide us with the means to dispatch Abraham Turner."

"I don't know, it still feels like gobbledygook to me." Mead shook his head. "You really think a golden knife smeared with a murder victim's blood is going to have any effect on that monster?"

"I guess we'll find out soon enough." Decker was walking toward the chip shop's rear door. When he tried the handle, the door swung inward into darkness.

"You'd have thought he would've locked it behind him if he's in there," Mead whispered, peering past Decker into the gloom.

"He must've been in a hurry. Maybe the ritual to steal a person's life force has a time limit. Wait too long and it doesn't work."

Mead glanced down the alley. "Or maybe he killed the woman and fled."

"Only one way to find out," Decker said, then he stepped across the threshold into the swirling darkness.

# FIFTY-FOUR

THE DARKNESS inside the chip shop was absolute. Decker took out his phone, then activated the flashlight. They were in a storeroom at the back of the shop. Metal racks filled the space, loaded with bottles of cooking oil, ketchup, vinegar, and assorted other food related items. One shelf contained stacks of disposable food containers. A set of stairs occupied one wall, leading to the upper floor where they had seen the lights blazing. When he aimed the flashlight down, Decker was horrified to see a smeared trail of dried blood leading from the rear door to a wall freezer on the other side of the room.

He followed the trail, a sick feeling resting in his gut. When he opened the freezer door, his worst fears were confirmed. A body lay slumped against the far wall. A portly man in his fifties with thinning hair and a white apron stained with blood. He was dead, his sightless eyes staring toward Decker. A coating of frost encrusted his pallid blue tinged skin. "Looks like he's been dead for a while," Decker said in a whisper. "Turner must've been using this for his hideout."

"There was a light on upstairs," Mead replied, taking in the grisly scene then glancing up toward the ceiling. "We have him trapped."

"Let's not take anything for granted." Decker went to the door leading into the front of the shop and looked around. As he suspected, it was empty. He crossed to the stairs and looked up. The door at the top was closed, a thin crack of light around its edges the only illumination. Decker started up, keeping his foot falls light. When he reached the top, Decker paused, his hand on the doorknob. He sensed Detective Inspector Mead at his rear. He could feel the knife in his jacket pocket, pressed against his chest. He took it out. Then he turned the knob and let the door swing inward.

The room was lit by a single floor lamp standing in the corner. A sofa stood against one wall. The remains of takeout food, mostly Chinese cartons, littered the coffee table. It appeared the chip shop owner was not big on his own cuisine.

Decker stepped over the threshold into the cramped living room. He gripped the knife tight, expecting to fend off an attack at any moment, but the space was empty. Mead entered behind him and went to the window. He glanced out toward the street, then turned back into the room.

There were two doors leading into the rest of the flat. One was a bathroom. The other was a bedroom. Decker could see the shape of a bed in the darkness beyond the open door. When he investigated, he found this room was empty too.

"I don't get it," Mead said. "I was sure he would be up here."

"He can't be far away." Decker made a cursory check of the bathroom, even though he could see that it was unoccupied. "We weren't that far behind him."

"He must've seen us coming and fled. What if he hijacked another car?"

"He still has the watch," Decker said. He turned off the phone's flashlight and brought up the GPS tracker again. Then he frowned. "According to this, we're right on top of him."

"That's impossible." Mead surveyed the room. "He's not here. There's nowhere to hide."

"Maybe he doesn't need to," Decker said. An uncomfortable thought had occurred to him. His eyes fell on the coffee table and a small metallic object sitting there. He crossed and picked it up, then held it between two fingers and showed Mead. "The GPS tracker."

"The bastard found it. How did he know?"

"He might be from another century, but he's smarter than even I gave him credit for." Decker felt a thud of disappointment. He'd made a dreadful mistake in handing the watch over to Abraham Turner. Now two people had paid the price for his miscalculation. His thoughts turned to Mina. More than likely she was already dead. He'd seen plenty of stabbings in his time, and very few people survived a wound to the chest. Her sacrifice had been for nothing.

"There's no more we can do here." Mead was heading toward the door. "I have a couple of victims to take care of. I'm going to call this in. Maybe forensics can find something useful."

"I doubt they'll have much luck." Abraham Turner had expected their every move. He could be anywhere by now. "But it's better than doing nothing."

Mead was at the head of the stairs now. He turned back to Decker. "You coming?"

"In a minute. I need to gather my thoughts."

"Fair enough," Mead said. Then he turned and descended the stairs.

Decker watched him go. He heard the detective inspector reach the bottom of the stairs and exit into the alley, closing the door behind him. Silence rushed in to fill the void. He thought about calling Colum, but hesitated, afraid of what the Irishman would tell him. He also didn't want to admit that Abraham Turner had escaped despite their best efforts. He glanced down at the knife still in his hand, smeared with the blood of both Mina and the middle-aged woman in the car outside. It was useless now.

He turned toward the door with a deep sigh. But as he did so, he noticed something on the ceiling above the coffee table. A square hatch with a panel that wasn't quite resting in place, a wedge of darkness showing through.

An attic.

Decker froze. Abraham Turner couldn't have known about the bug in his watch before he arrived back here. If he had, he would have discarded it somewhere else rather than lead them straight to his hideout. He only thought to check the watch when he realized that they had found him. The likelihood was that he didn't even know what the tracker actually was. All he knew was that it did not belong inside his watch. He made a leap of logic and assumed it was the means by which Decker had tracked him. Decker felt a surge of hope. If Turner didn't realize they had found him until they reached the chip shop, he could not have escaped. He had removed the tracker and left it for them to find, hoping they would assume he was long gone. But he wasn't. He was hiding in the one place they hadn't thought to look. It had almost worked. Mead had left and returned to the police car. Decker had been about to follow him.

Decker stared at the opening and cursed under his breath. If he called out to the detective, it would alert Abraham of his suspicions.

He would have to deal with Abraham Turner on his own.

Decker eyed the coffee table, wondering whether the piece of dilapidated furniture would support his weight. There was only one way to find out. He stepped upon it and reached up, sliding the panel back. Then he gripped the edges of the hole and hauled himself into the dark attic.

# FIFTY-FIVE

DECKER PULLED himself up and swung his legs into the cramped space under the building's roof. He clambered to his feet, finding himself standing in an open area between V-shaped support beams that held the sloping roof in place. The attic extended away from him in both directions, falling into unfathomable blackness. There was little room to maneuver apart from a four-foot-wide strip that ran down its center. Decker turned his phone's flashlight back on. In his other hand, he gripped the knife.

He stepped away from the attic entrance and lifted the phone to scan his surroundings. He swept the flashlight in a wide circle; the beam picking out cardboard boxes thick with dust, a couple of old paintings in dilapidated frames leaning against a vertical support beam, and an old tennis racket hanging from a rusty nail. The walls at each end of the attic were thick with cobwebs. More cobwebs hung over head. Decker took a step further away from the entrance, pushing the flashlight beam further into the gloom. It picked up more boxes, stacked two and three high. It also illuminated something else.

A shape crouched in the furthest corner, watching him.

Then, before Decker had time to prepare, the shape lunged forward. Abraham Turner, head lowered, hit him square in the chest and sent Decker staggering backwards. The phone fell from his grip and skittered off across the floor, the flashlight extinguishing as it did so.

Decker regained his feet and turned in the darkness, unsure from where the next attack would occur. Out of the blackness, a voice floated.

"It's no use, I'm stronger than you."

"We'll see about that," Decker said, his ears straining to pick up the direction from which the voice came.

A chuckle reached his ears, maniacal and chilling.

Decker swiveled, sensing movement behind him.

Turner crashed into him again, and Decker saw the flash of a knife. He tried to bring his own knife to bear, even as he felt the Ripper's blade slice into his shoulder. He let out a pained grunt and slashed the darkness, but Turner had retreated once more. He felt warm blood trickling down his arm, but he appeared to still have full movement. The cut felt bad, but it had caused no major damage.

Decker hunkered lower and waited for the next attack. He could see nothing in the darkness, unlike Turner, who apparently had no such problem thanks to whatever unnatural source his vampiric abilities sprang from. He didn't have to wait long. There was a rush of air and then Abraham Turner was upon him, attacking from the rear and dragging him backwards into the gloom. Decker thrashed and tried to turn. He stabbed blindly with the knife but could not find his mark. He felt a surge of panic. If he didn't do something soon, Turner would cut his throat for sure. Decker would be as dead as the woman in the car behind the chip shop. In a last-ditch effort to gain the advantage and praying the Ripper's own weapon would not impale him, Decker let himself fall backwards into Turner.

They tumbled to the floor, entwined in each other. Decker struggled to stand up before Turner regained his wits and finished him. Just as he was climbing to his feet, he heard a sharp crack. The floor shifted and buckled. Then, with a mighty groan, the attic floorboards, rotten from years of neglect, gave way beneath them. The next moment they were falling through the ceiling in a shower of plaster and splintered wood.

Decker braced himself for a hard landing, but found his fall cushioned by soft fabric instead. The couch was directly beneath them and had absorbed much of the tumble's impact. The knife though, which he'd been clutching as the floor gave way, was no longer in his grip, jarred from his hand as he fell. It now lay on the other side of the coffee table, out of reach. Next to him, Abraham Turner was regaining his feet, his own knife still tightly clutched.

Decker felt a whoosh of air as the blade zipped past him, too close for comfort. He ducked and rolled sideways, knocking the coffee table aside and landed on the floor, then scrambled forward to reclaim his own weapon. His hand closed around the hilt just as Turner advanced and brought the knife down to skewer him.

Decker rolled sideways, but not fast enough. The blade nicked his ribs, sending fresh waves of pain coursing through him. He skittered backwards and regained his feet near the window, back to the wall. Now he got his first good look at Abraham Turner since the man fled, and it shocked him. Turner was nothing like the dried-up walking corpse that met him in Hyde Park. His skin glowed with the vigor of youth. His eyes were bright. His hair flowed thick and dark. If Decker hadn't known better, he would've said that Turner wasn't a day over thirty years of age.

"This is all thanks to your young friend," Turner said, relishing the look of horror on Decker's face. "And the woman in the car, of course, although she had less years ahead of her. Still, one takes what one can get."

"Mina." Decker said the word quietly, more to himself than to his adversary. "You killed her."

"It was nothing personal," Turner said, making no attempt to advance upon Decker. Knowing he had the upper hand. "She was brimming with youth, and I had a lot of time to make up for. If it's any consolation, I can feel her life force flowing within, giving me strength. I can sense her memories, the fondness she had for you."

Decker felt a chill run up his spine. "You know nothing about her."

"Oh, but I do. I know all about your little friend, Mina. That's a perk of stealing lives. She thought you'd protect her. She thought you'd keep her safe. It's pathetic really." Abraham Turner's lips curled up into a vicious grin. "But not at the end. She hated you as she drowned in her own mortality. She cursed you with her dying breath."

"No. That's not true." Decker fought back a choking sob.

"Believe what you will," Turner said, taking a step forward. He raised the knife. "You'll be able to ask her in person soon. Once I'm finished with you."

"Don't come any closer," Decker said, showing Turner the golden blade.

"What do you think you're going to do with that?" Turner laughed. "It won't work. I'll just pull it free and walk out of here. Gold alone does nothing."

"Except that Finch left me a message," Decker said. "He told me all about your Achilles heel. The gold has to be combined with your victim's blood."

"Ah, the blood." Abraham acknowledged. "It still won't stop me though. Abberline was smart. He knew it wouldn't work instantly, so he used gold dust to slow me down. Sprayed it in my face. I was blinded, couldn't get it off. All you have is a knife. Even with the blood on it, I'll just pull it right back out. Then I'll finish you. But not quickly. I'm going to make it hurt."

Decker gazed frantically around the room, desperate to find a means of escape, but there was none. He was trapped. Any moment now Turner would end his life just like he'd snuffed out Mina's and so many others. He braced himself for what was to come. He had failed his mission. He had failed Colum and Adam Hunt. Worst of all, he had failed Mina. Now he was going to pay the price.

# FIFTY-SIX

JOHN DECKER STOOD FACING Abraham Turner and prepared to meet his end. He tightened his grip on the golden blade, vowing that if he had to die, he would at least inflict some damage on his attacker.

Abraham observed him in the same way a cat might watch a cornered mouse. He was in no hurry. His confidence radiated from eyes as cold as stone. Decker had the feeling his adversary had faced down stronger men than he and lived to tell the tale.

A moment later, as if he'd grown bored with the game, Abraham took another step forward, his gaze never wavering from the object of his hatred.

Decker steeled himself for a final confrontation he could not win. Then, just when he thought there was no hope, Detective Inspector Mead appeared in the doorway behind them, a tire iron in hand.

"Hey," he shouted. "Why don't we make this a fair fight."

Abraham paused mid-stride, disbelief flashing across his face. He turned toward Mead. "I thought you had run away already."

"Yeah, well, I didn't." Mead raised the tire iron. He glanced past Abraham. "Now would be a good time."

Decker was way ahead of him. The momentary distraction had

provided the opening Decker was waiting for. He lifted his arm and took aim, then threw the knife. It hung in the air, making a full rotation as it flew, the gold's weight causing the weapon to drop lower as it went. For one terrifying moment Decker thought the knife would drop short, but it didn't.

Abraham turned, sensing the attack, but in doing so presented a larger target. He raised his arms in defense a moment before the blade found his chest. It sank deep to the hilt.

Abraham's eyes narrowed. A smile creased his lips. He lifted a hand and gripped the knife, ready to pull it free. But then something strange happened. He gasped and let go of the handle. A glow pulsed around the blade, faint at first but getting brighter. It spread in all directions, igniting into a slow burning fire that swept across Abraham's chest like a thousand sparklers set off all at once. He screeched and dropped to his knees; the smug expression replaced by horror.

"What have you done to me," he gasped, looking up at Decker. "How is this possible?"

The fire was spreading now, burning white hot. Crackling sparks played over his body as if his very skin was alive with electricity.

Then his youth faded. His skin shriveled back upon his bones. His hair, newly thickened and luxurious, withered away to dusty gray clumps.

He let out a screech of rage and attempted to stand, but his legs would not carry his weight and he fell forward, smashing face first into the ground and driving the knife deeper still. He pushed himself up on his elbows, crawled toward Decker, even as the lightning that danced over his body flickered and faded. He lay there, a smoking charred husk, yet still somehow living. His mouth opened and closed but no words came out, vocal cords atrophied and useless. He raised a hand, reaching out toward the man that moments ago he wanted to kill. Then his arm dropped to his side and a rattling cough escaped his throat.

Finally, just when Decker thought the pyrotechnics were over, one last spark flickered across Abraham Turner's ruined body. It danced across his blackened skin and leaped upward in a mighty bolt of lightning that played across the ceiling, sending even more plaster and woodwork crashing down. The air itself came alive with electricity. Decker felt the hairs on the back of his arms stand up. And then it dissipated, returning to the ether as if it had never been there.

Of Abraham Turner, there was nothing left, but a charred pile of ash within which lay two knives, one glinting gold, the other old and tarnished, and a fob watch.

Detective Inspector Mead remained in the doorway; the tire iron still raised for an attack that would never come.

Decker touched a hand to his bleeding shoulder and winced. The wound was bad, but he would live. Then his thoughts turned to Colum and Mina. He'd lost his phone somewhere in the dark attic above, but now he saw it laying amid a pile of rubble near the sofa. It appeared to be undamaged. He stepped over what remained of Abraham Turner and picked it up, then called Colum. The least he could do was let the man know Mina had not died in vain, even though he was still unsure why the gold blade had produced such an extreme and instant effect.

"It's done. Turner is dead," he said when Colum answered. There would be time for explanations later, once Decker had figured out what happened, and why.

Colum drew in a long breath. When he spoke, it wasn't to acknowledge Decker's words. "Thank God you called, John. I'm not quite sure how to tell you this, but something's happened. It's Mina. We're at the hospital. You need to get over to Saint Mary's right now."

"What's going on?" Decker asked, cold dread tightening his chest. He knew it was unlikely she had survived, but he didn't want to hear the words. But putting it off would not lessen the blow. He braced himself for bad news. "Is Mina dead?"

"No," Colum said. "I don't know how. But she's alive."

Relief flooded over Decker. "Thank goodness. What is it then?"

Colum paused before he answered. "I think it's better you see for yourself. Just get here as quickly as you can."

# FIFTY-SEVEN

FOR THE SECOND time that night, they drove through London's darkened streets in a mad dash. This time though, Detective Inspector Mead used the siren and the lights.

"How am I going to explain this to my superiors?" Mead said with a shake of his head. "It's freaking nuts."

"I'm sure you'll think of something," Decker replied. Colum's words reverberated in his head. A writhing ball of fear sat in his stomach like a coiling snake. Mina was still alive, and that was good news. But why was Colum unwilling to elaborate? What could have happened to her that was worse than being stabbed in the chest?

The car flew along, this time having no problem navigating the roads. The siren was enough to move any slowpokes. After a ten-minute ride, they pulled up outside the accident and emergency entrance of St. Mary's Hospital in Westminster. Decker barely waited for the car to come to a halt before he jumped out, sprinting toward the hospital doors. On the other side of the waiting room a nurse sat behind a desk tapping away on the computer. Detective Inspector Mead was a few steps behind Decker. They made their way toward the nurse. She glanced up, an irritated look on her face, as if they shouldn't be there. But when Mead pulled out his warrant card her demeanor changed. He was about to speak when a commotion drew their attention.

"Decker!"

He recognized the voice instantly. He could hardly believe his eyes.

It was Mina.

She was approaching from a corridor that led off the waiting room, coat zipped up to her chin. Colum followed behind, accompanied by two doctors and a nurse. All four looked harried.

Decker rushed toward her.

She flung her arms around him. "I never thought I'd see you again."

"Me either," Decker said, wincing as pain flared in his shoulder.

"I'm so sorry," Mina released him, staring in horror at his bloodied shirt. you're hurt."

"Turner got me with his knife. It's a flesh wound," Decker reassured her.

"You need to get it looked at."

"All in good time," Decker said. There were more urgent matters. "How are you here? You were dying."

"Not anymore." Mina grinned. "I'm all better."

"That's impossible," Decker said. He took a step back and looked at her. Mina's eyes were full of life, her skin flushed with vigor. "I saw Abraham Turner sink a knife into your chest. I watched you fade away."

"I know," Mina said. "I remember being stabbed. The pain was incredible. Then it all gets hazy. I have recollections of saying goodbye to you, of being in the ambulance. Then I woke up in an operating room surrounded by doctors. Boy, were they surprised. You'd have thought they'd seen me come back from the dead."

"They did," Colum said. "We got her to the hospital and I'm telling you, John, she was close to dead. There was barely a pulse, and she wasn't responsive. They wheeled her right into the operating room, but no one thought she'd survive. The next thing I know, there's a hell of a commotion. She's on her feet and trying to leave. And get this. The doctors claim that a bolt of lightning came through the ceiling and revived her. Her stab wound went away, just like that. Healed in front of their eyes like it was never there."

"I've never seen anything like it," one doctor said, shaking his head. "I've seen some miraculous things in my time, but no one's ever healed themselves in front of my eyes. Not like that."

"You and Abraham Turner were still connected," Decker said thoughtfully. He remembered the bolt of lightning that had leaped from Turner's body at the end. How it disappeared into the ceiling. Now he realized it had done so much more. "When I stabbed Turner with the gold knife, it must've been like throwing a switch and putting the whole process into reverse. He didn't know it, but you weren't quite dead yet. There was still a tether between you. All the energy that he was stealing from you flowed back the other way. That's why the knife had such an effect. Instead of draining your life force, you drained his. You literally sucked him dry."

"Turned him to dust," Mead said. "It was an incredible sight."

"You need to go back with the doctors and get checked out," Colum said to Mina.

"I'm fine," Mina protested. "Good as new. Not even a scratch. It would've been nice if they kept my blouse though, ripped and bloodstained or not. Then I wouldn't need to have this coat zipped to my chin. It's a shame. I really liked that blouse. I'd only worn twice."

"I'll buy you a new one," Decker said. "Hell, I'll buy ten of them. We'll go on a shopping spree whenever you're feeling up to it. I'm sure Adam Hunt can splurge for a trip to Regent Street."

"Now hold on a minute," Colum said. "My expense account isn't that big."

"Mina literally died for us," Decker said. "We wouldn't have stopped Abraham Turner without her. I think it's a fair exchange." He turned back to Mina. "What do you say?"

"Sounds fantastic," Mina replied with a grin. "But can it wait a few days? My stab wound might have healed, but I still remember what it was like."

"Sure. Whenever you're ready." Decker looked at Colum. "She

seems fine to me. I see no reason to put her through more stress. If she doesn't want to stay here, I see no reason to force her."

"She was dying less than an hour ago." Colum didn't look happy.

"But I'm not dying now," Mina said. "In fact, I feel better than ever. I don't think I've ever felt this much energy. I'm not going back with those doctors, and that's the all there is to it."

"Mina…" Colum protested.

"I mean it, I'm fine." Mina nodded toward Decker's shoulder. "You're not though. We're taking care of that wound. Right now. No arguments."

# FIFTY-EIGHT

THREE DAYS later Decker sat in the Reardon Grand Hotel's bar with Colum and Mina. Adam Hunt, concerned for the girl's ongoing health, had instructed them to stay and monitor her, which they had done with glee. A few more days in London was no hardship.

Colum eyed the remains of their first round of drinks, three empty glasses. "I'll get us some refills," he said, slipping from the booth and picking up the empties.

Mina watched him go, then she turned to Decker. "I need to talk to you. I didn't want to say anything in front of Colum. I don't want this getting back to Adam Hunt."

"You can trust Colum," Decker said.

"I'd rather this stay between the two of us, at least for now," Mina replied. "Things have been weird the last few days and I'm not sure what to think."

"Weird?" Decker felt a jolt of concern. "Are you feeling unwell? We really don't know what the side effects of your experience will be. If something is wrong, then we need to get you help."

"It's not that anything is wrong," Mina said. "It's more that I feel different. It's like I'm me, but I'm also not. Every night since Abraham Turner died, I've had dreams. But they feel like so much more. They are more like memories. I was on a battlefield in ancient times, walking among the dead looking for wounded warriors to steal their life force. I was a witch finder in the Middle Ages."

"It's probably just your unconscious mind trying to deal with the trauma. I'm sure it will pass."

"No. It's more than that. I feel it when I'm awake too." Mina shook her head. She looked worried. "I felt it the minute I woke up on the operating table. When you killed Abraham Turner, stabbed him with that knife, all of his energy flowed back the other way. I could feel it pouring into me. Filling me. All his memories, all his experiences. A thousand years of existence ripped from him and dropped inside of me. I remember everything. It's like a part of him is inside of me, living on, but it doesn't feel like a life I lived. It feels more like a vivid dream." Mina paused, gathering her thoughts. "Actually, it's more like a nightmare."

"I'm so sorry," Decker said.

"The things he did. The pain he inflicted. It's horrible." Mina's voice quivered. "It's weird. Jack the Ripper used to fascinate me. Now I have all his memories. I know what he did to every one of those women, how they suffered. I looked into their eyes as they died. There are so many more too. Women whose names the world will never know."

"Not you. Him. Those memories aren't your own. Remember that."

"Doesn't make it any easier."

"I know." Decker shook his head. "It's awful."

"I'll learn to live with it," Mina said. "If I focus on other things, it fades into the background. There are moments when I forget it's even there, at least consciously. To tell you the truth, the memories aren't the thing that scares me the most."

"What is?" Decker asked.

"This." Mina extended her arm across the table and pulled her sleeve up. She showed Decker her wrist, and the symbol burned into it. "It appeared after I left the hospital. At first it was faint. I could barely see it. When I woke up the next day, it looked like this."

"You have the same mark Abraham Turner carried." Decker felt a tug of despair. What had he done to Mina?

"Yes. I've become like him."

"Not like him. You could never become like him. You aren't a monster."

"I know." Mina nodded. "The thing is, he didn't just steal my life force that night. He killed that woman in her car and absorbed her years too. When the process reversed, it not only returned the stolen decades of own life, but it gave me Abraham Turner's as well, and that of the murdered woman. I can sense her memories, just as I sense his. There are so many minds living inside of me now, or at least the ghosts of them. All his victims. Some recollections are stronger than others, but they are all there."

"I don't know what to say."

"You don't have to say anything. I would like you to give me an honest answer, though. If I'm like him now, did my own life get extended by the years he took from that poor woman in the car?" Mina leaned closer to Decker. "How long am I going to live?"

"I can't answer that." Decker sighed. "Only time will tell."

"That's what I thought," Mina said. She forced a smile and touched Decker's hand. "No matter what, I'm still me. I'll deal with this like I've dealt with everything else."

"I know you will." Decker returned the smile.

At that moment Colum returned carrying three drinks. He placed them on the table and slipped back into the booth. "Did I miss anything interesting?"

"Not much," Mina said, reaching for her drink. The concern had left her face now. The mask was back on. "So, tell me, what does Adam Hunt have in store for you guys next? I bet it's going to be really cool."

# EPILOGUE

## ONE WEEK LATER

IT WAS nine at night and the sun was slipping low on the horizon in a fiery blaze of reds and yellows as John Decker arrived back at the rented house that he and Nancy shared in the flat marshlands of Gulf Coast, Mississippi. Twelve hours earlier he had bid a sad farewell to Mina with the promise that he would call her often. He'd stayed on several extra days after Colum departed for Dublin, concerned for her wellbeing. But he could not stay forever, and this morning he'd given Mina one last hug and boarded a direct flight from London's Heathrow to Louis Armstrong International in New Orleans. After he deplaned, a driver was waiting courtesy of Adam Hunt, and before he knew it, they left the airport behind on the way to his home some fifty miles distant.

He approached the front steps with his bag over one shoulder, weary and drained. The front door wasn't locked. He stepped inside and dropped his bag in the hallway, expecting to find Nancy there waiting for him, but she wasn't. From deeper within the house, the strains of jazz music reached his ears. John Coltrane. One of his favorites. He followed the dulcet tones along the hallway and into the kitchen. The lighting was low. Candles flickered on the kitchen counters. There were more on the small dining room table. There was also a bottle of wine and two glasses, both half full. Nancy stood in the doorway between the kitchen and living room. She wore a sexy little black dress. Her hair was down, cascading over her shoulders. Her soft eyes glinted in the candle's warm light.

"Welcome home," she said, her voice low and sultry. "It's been so lonely here without you."

"I bet you hardly missed me," Decker replied. He stepped into the kitchen. "You probably spent every day since getting back from Florida watching sappy movies on the Hallmark Channel."

"I always miss you." Nancy met him halfway across the kitchen floor. She put her arms around him and kissed him. "I poured us some wine."

"I see that." Decker held her close. Nancy's hair smelled like sweet jasmine. When she pulled away, he spoke again, motioning toward the candles and the wine. "You didn't have to do this just because I'm home."

"I wanted to." Nancy picked up a wine glass and offered it to him, then took her own. "I also wanted to talk to you. There's something I need to say."

"That sounds ominous." A memory of the two of them up at the water hole in Florida pushed its way into his mind. How he'd asked her to marry him, and she had turned him down. "This isn't your way of breaking up with me, is it?"

"Heavens, no." Nancy looked aghast. "Is that what you think this is?"

Decker shrugged. "I don't know. Maybe."

"If I was ending things with you, the last thing I would do is light candles and pour wine, you silly man. Actually, it's entirely the opposite. I know how much it hurt you when I didn't say yes to your marriage proposal. It was just so sudden. I'd only just escaped being eaten by a prehistoric alligator. It took me by surprise."

"I know that," Decker said. "And I'm willing to give you the time that you need. However long it takes. I'll be here for you. I'll be waiting."

"That's just it. I don't want more time. These last two weeks away from you have been so hard. I know I can't have you with me all the time, but I'd rather pine for my husband than my boyfriend."

"Are you saying…"

"I'm saying yes." Nancy's gaze met his. "I want to marry you and I'm sorry I didn't say that two weeks ago when you first asked me."

Decker stood and looked at her. He put the wineglass aside. Moments ticked by.

"For goodness' sake, say something." Nancy bit her bottom lip. "You're scaring me. You do still want to marry me?"

"More than anything," Decker said. "I was just savoring the moment, that's all."

Nancy threw her arms around him again. She kissed him. "Why don't we both savor this moment."

"Sounds good to me," Decker said. He wrapped his arms around her and held her tight. He closed his eyes and wished they could stay like that forever.

Then his phone buzzed.

"Don't you dare look at that," Nancy whispered in his ear. She nuzzled into his neck, her hair tickling his skin.

"It might be important."

"It always is." Nancy stroked the back of his neck.

"I'll ignore it."

"It's killing you, not knowing what that text message says, isn't it?" Nancy asked with a laugh.

"Little bit."

"Go on then. Take a peek."

Decker reached into his pocket with one hand and pulled his phone out. He glanced at the screen then put the phone away again.

"Well?" Nancy asked. "What did it say?"

"It was Adam Hunt."

"I figured that much."

"It said, have you ever been on a German U-boat?"

"Absolutely not." Nancy pulled her head away from Decker's shoulder and glared at him. "You're not disappearing to go fight some creepy monster on a U-boat. Not yet. You've only just arrived home. You tell him I want a week with my future husband before he drags you off to battle Frankenstein's Monster, or the Abominable Snowman, or Nazi super-soldiers on some secret submarine."

"Okay, I'll tell him." Decker reached for his phone again.

"What are you doing? Not right at this moment." Nancy disengaged and put her hands on her hips. She glanced toward the bedroom. "Adam Hunt can wait. I can't."

Decker smiled. He picked up his wineglass and watched Nancy head off toward the bedroom. He lingered a moment, overcome with happiness, then he took the phone out of his pocket, turned it off, and followed her.

**READ ON FOR AN EXCERPT FROM THE NEXT JOHN DECKER BOOK—BLACK TIDE.**

## FEBRUARY 1943

The Avro Lancaster bomber sliced through the frigid deep winter night on the way to Frankfurt, flying near its altitude ceiling of a little over 24,000 feet to avoid anti-aircraft fire. To the left and right, more bombers flew in tight formation, while below, the Belgian countryside slipped by unseen thanks to a thick layer of cloud cover. In the pilot's seat, Flt. Lt. Ernest Latimer stared out uneasily into the pitch-black sky. They had left the relative safety of the English Channel far behind and would now be vulnerable to attack by Luftwaffe interceptors. But only if the Germans detected them, which Ernest hoped would not happen, at least until they dropped their payload. At that point, the element of surprise would be lost, and all bets were off. But for now, everything was quiet.

"I saw Betty last night," said the flight engineer, Sgt. Frank Ward, from the second dickie seat to Ernest's right. "She was in a mood, I'll tell you. She could barely keep her hands off me when I walked her home. Let me kiss her and everything. She always gets like that before a sortie. Keen as mustard. I swear, it's like she doesn't think she'll ever see me again."

"What have I told you about talking like that." Ernest glared at the flight engineer. "It's bad luck."

"I was just stating a fact. It's true. She gets all worried every time there's a mission. Besides, nothing's going to happen. We'll come home safe and sound just like always. Best bomber crew in the squadron, we are."

"Luck. That's all it is. We've shared the skies with plenty of crews that didn't make it home."

"Long may that luck hold." Frank sniffed and wiped his nose with the back of his hand. "To tell the truth, I thought it would all be over by now. Who knew the Krauts would be this persistent. I figured a few months of fighting, a year tops, and they'd throw their hands up. It's a shame they didn't learn their lesson after the last time we gave 'em a good hiding. It'll be four years this September. It's getting tiresome, I'll tell you."

"What else have you got to do?" asked Ernest.

"I suppose." Frank chuckled. "The RAF would be a pretty good flying club if it wasn't for those pesky Messerschmitts." He lapsed into silence and studied his own reflection in the cockpit window. At last, he spoke again. "I think I might ask Betty to marry me."

"Now why would you want to go and do a harebrained thing like that?" Now it was Ernest's turn to chuckle. "The skirts love a man in uniform."

"Especially if that uniform's American," Frank retorted.

"You're not wrong there, lad." A new voice drifted from beyond the curtain blocking off the navigator's station. The fabric swished back to reveal Tommy Corker, otherwise known as Fish, not because he liked to swim, but because of his ability to sink pints at the Kings Arms, which was legendary. He sat perched at the chart table, crammed between the cockpit and the wireless operator's station. Above him the astrodome, used for celestial navigation, was nothing but a dark hole in the plane's fuselage. "It's bloody impossible to pull when the Yanks are in the pub, and since they only fly daytime raids, they're always in the pub."

"Which is why I'm sticking with Betty," Frank said. "It's just easier."

"And because you love her too, right?" Tommy shook his head, bewildered.

"Well, yes, there is that."

"Spoken like a true romantic." Ernest glanced back at the navigator. "Are we close?"

"We're over the German border and in the rats' nest." The joviality had fallen from Tommy's face. He now looked scared. "Almost on top of it."

The seven-man crew fell silent, their concentration now focused on the job at hand. To complete the bombing run, they would have to break cloud cover. Ernest closed the throttles and allowed the plane to start its descent in anticipation of the Master Bomber's orders. Below them would be small villages and towns, while up ahead sat Frankfurt. Their target. He could see the other bombers following suit and dropping lower as they prepared to release their payloads of 500lb bombs. One plane flew too close, threatening to drop right on top of them, and Ernest jabbed his left rudder with a curse. The Lancaster reacted, pulling away at the last minute and avoiding a midair collision.

"Phew. That was a close one," Ernest said, wiping a sheen of sweat from his forehead.

"I swear, they're giving the new pilots less and less training." Tommy looked up from the chart table. "I know we're short of men and all, but they should at least give them an eyesight test before putting them in the cockpit."

"I blame the Germans myself," Ernest replied. "If only they'd be good sports and stop shooting us down, we wouldn't need new pilots."

"Chaps, were not out of the woods yet." Frank was looking up through the cockpit canopy from his lower position in the collapsible seat next to the pilot. His eyes were wide with surprise. "There's something coming down toward us. I've never seen anything like it."

"Stone the crows." Ernest followed the flight engineer's gaze and for a moment he could not comprehend what he was looking at. Above them, dropping out of the moonless sky, was a spherical red orb. "What in blazes is that?"

"I wish I knew." Frank shifted in his seat, nervous, as the orb dropped closer.

"You think it's a new German weapon? Some kind of defense system?" Tommy was craning his neck to see. He stood and pushed his head into the astrodome to get a better view. As he did so, the glowing red orb drew level with their aircraft.

It stayed that way for a few seconds, matching their course and airspeed, and then without warning, shot off at ninety degrees, weaving in and out of the tightly packed planes at impossible speed.

Ernest held his breath, waiting for the sphere to impact one of the forward bombers and send it crashing to the ground in flames. But it didn't. Instead, the unusual object pulled ahead of the squadron, turned, and shot straight up into the firmament where it disappeared from view.

"It's gone." Tommy dropped back down into the cabin and took his seat again. "A pretty useless secret weapon, if you ask me."

"Maybe not. We have more company coming straight for us," Ernest said, watching the Lancaster ahead of them billow into a sudden ball of flames and spiral downward, leaving a bright orange streak as it headed into oblivion. "And this time there's no doubt who they are and what they want."

"Night fighters." Frank's voice was laced with fear. The dreaded Luftwaffe BF 109 Messerschmitt's were equipped with radar, allowing them to see the incoming bombers before they even knew there was a problem. That, coupled with their superior armaments, made them a formidable foe. "If we don't get out of the way, we won't stand a chance. The buggers will shoot us to pieces before we even get a look in."

"Already taking care of it." Ernest pulled back on the stick. The plane's nose lifted, taking them back up and out of the line of fire. His heart began to beat slower and for a few seconds he thought they had avoided trouble even as the bombers that remained at lower altitude were being swiftly picked off, their gunners unable to find the marauding defenders thanks to a combination of darkness and the longer range of the German guns.

But then Tommy was leaping up again and peering through the astrodome's spherical glass. "I don't want to worry you, fellows, but that red ball is back, and it's brought some friends along."

Ernest peered upward to see the glowing red orb dropping back toward them, surrounded by four more pulsating spheres. They raced downward toward the fray, zigzagging between the aircraft, and making sharp turns that would have ripped a regular plane apart. "That nails it. They must be some sort of weapon."

"I don't know," Frank said. "I've heard the American fly boys talking in the pub. They've seen them too. They call them foo fighters.

They've shown up even when the Germans aren't around, and they certainly aren't ours."

"Whatever they are, they're getting in the way." Ernest pushed on the stick to avoid an orb that had dropped directly in their path. The plane's nose dipped, and the orb slid momentarily upward, out of view. Below them, more of the incandescent balls were streaking in and out of the bombers still at a lower altitude, hampering their efforts to fend off the attacking fighter planes.

"Look out." Frank's eyes flew wide with terror. He pointed thirty degrees down and to their left.

Ernest followed the engineer's gaze and saw, to his horror, an ominous shape flitting through the darkness below them. The unmistakable outline of an ME-110. If it got under them, it would use its upward facing 20mm cannons to rip into the now defenseless Lancaster's belly.

He did the only thing he could. He pulled hard on the stick and pushed the plane back upward in a fast ascent, just as the Messerschmitt opened up. Bullets streaked through the sky. A curtain of death that advanced as the enemy aircraft drew near. But that was not the worst of it. The orb that Ernest had tried so hard to avoid was too close. Even with its greater maneuverability, it was caught off guard by the Lancaster's sudden course change, and the German bullets that slammed into it from below.

The orb's pulsating red light filled bomber's the cockpit.

Ernest let out a strangled cry.

He made a frantic attempt to turn the plane to the right and avoid a collision. But it was too little, too late. The bomber's wing tipped up as the plane banked. It smacked into the sphere, which was not as amorphous as it initially appeared. An engine flared up. Part of the wing tore away and dropped out of sight.

For a terrible moment, time ground to a halt.

Ernest glanced at his engineer, saw the terror on his face.

The rear gunner screamed as rounds from the Messerschmitt tore through their fuselage and peppered him.

Tommy cried out, a desperate prayer escaping his lips as the realization of their predicament dawned upon him.

Then the Lancaster's nose dropped one last time and the plane, unable to keep level flight with half a wing missing, twisted sideways and fell in a sickening, lurching spiral.

Ernest gripped the stick and fought to right the stricken bomber, but it was useless. While next to them like some aerobatic dance partner was the orb—red glow fading now to reveal a spherical metallic craft, the likes of which Ernest had never seen—accompanying them into oblivion.

---

Dawn. Smoke hung over the field, acrid and black. A deep trough cut through the landscape, starting near a copse of fir trees and ending at the shattered remains of an Allied bomber half-buried in the earth near a narrow winding stream.

Gunter Lang and his son, Elias, trudged across the muddy pasture, which was still wet from an earlier rainstorm. In his hand Gunter carried a pitchfork. He didn't think anyone would still be alive inside the burned and broken plane, but he wasn't taking any chances. As they drew close, he quickened his pace and took up a position ahead of his son, shielding him just in case. But there was no need. The bomber had all but disintegrated on impact. The tail section, including the shattered gunner's position, lay twenty feet from the main wreckage. A wing had clipped the ground and come free, tumbling end over end and landing in the stream, propellers bent back upon themselves. The cockpit was unrecognizable. Nothing but a mass of tangled metal. The fuselage was buckled, its back broken. A dead airman hung from the open side door as if his lifeless body had tried to escape its own horrific end.

Gunter relaxed a little. There was no danger here beyond the obvious hazards of torn metal and spilled fuel. Or so he thought until he saw the second object sitting upright in a shallow crater a little further away.

A chill wormed its way up Gunter's spine.

This was like nothing he had ever seen. It was a perfect sphere, with what looked like geometric patterns etched across its surface. It was large too. At least twenty feet tall.

He approached the strange orb and stopped short, peering up at it. Beside him, his son let out a gasp.

"What it is?"

"I don't know." Gunter rubbed his chin. "Never saw anything like it."

"We should go now." Elias took a step backwards.

"Not yet." Gunter inched forward. His foot slid at the edge of the crater. He steadied himself, then turned to his son. "Stay here."

"Papa, don't go down there." Elias looked scared. "Please?"

"There's nothing to worry about, I promise. I'll be back in a moment." Gunter steeled himself, then stepped into the crater, skittering down the slope amid a cascade of loose rocks and soil. Everywhere else, the ground was soaked. Here, it was dry, the rain vaporized by the intense heat when the object crashed to earth.

Gunter was at the sphere now. He reached out, touched a palm to it. Felt a throbbing pulse from within. Something was running deep inside the orb. He pulled his hand away, surprised. Then he heard a rumble of engines. Shouts. He turned, just in time to see his son at the edge of the crater, flanked by men in dark uniforms, twin lightning rod patches sewn to their sleeves.

The Waffen-SS. Heinrich Himmler's dreaded elite troopers.

They aimed their guns downward into the pit.

He swallowed hard and raised his arms, eyes flitting between the soldiers and his terrified son. If they were lucky, he and Elias would live to see another dawn.

# ACKNOWLEDGMENTS

I would like to thank my friend, DI Neil Meade, for his invaluable advice that made the police procedural aspects of this novel more realistic. I took some liberties with that advice anyway, in the name of art, and for that I offer my humble apologies. I would also like to say a big thank you to my VIP team, who spot the occasional typo, give me feedback, and make the books so much better. Lastly, I would like thank my wife, Sonya, who wishes I wrote anything but monsters, but still edits my books and tells me to go back and do it again when I get lazy.

# ABOUT THE AUTHOR

Anthony M. Strong is a British-born writer living and working in the United States. He is the author of the popular John Decker series of supernatural adventure thrillers.

Anthony has worked as a graphic designer, newspaper writer, artist, and actor. When he was a young boy, he dreamed of becoming an Egyptologist and spent hours reading about pyramids and tombs. Until he discovered dinosaurs and decided to be a paleontologist instead. Neither career panned out, but he was left with a fascination for monsters and archaeology that serve him well in the John Decker books.

Anthony has traveled extensively across Europe and the United States, and weaves his love of travel into his novels, setting them both close to home and in far-off places.

Anthony currently resides most of the year on Florida's Space Coast where he can watch rockets launch from his balcony, and part of the year on an island in Maine, with his wife Sonya, and two furry bosses, Izzie and Hayden.

Connect with Anthony, find out about new releases, and get free books at www.anthonymstrong.com

www.ingramcontent.com/pod-product-compliance
Lightning Source LLC
Chambersburg PA
CBHW020501310726
48979CB00016B/2745/J
*9781942207146*